PRAISE FOR
WITHDRAWN

The Mad Wolf's Daughter

A *NEW YORK TIMES* EDITORS' CHOICE
KIDS' INDIE NEXT LIST PICK

"[A] **master storyteller** . . . feels like an instant classic."
—Soman Chainani, author of the
School for Good and Evil series

★ "Empathetic, bold, and entirely herself at a time when women were dismissed as weak, Drest shines in this **fast-paced adventure**." —*Publishers Weekly,* starred review

"Action-packed at every turn." —*Kirkus Reviews*

"**Cliffhanger chapter endings** keep the reader engaged . . . This book should have wide gender appeal." —VOYA

"I loved it. A **heart-warming and heart-pounding** adventure."
—Karen Cushman, Newbery Honor–winning author

"[Drest is] the **best type of hero**: striving to be kind and just, even when "right" and "wrong" are hard to define."
—Kristen Cashore, *New York Times* bestselling author

"A **gripping adventure** with a marvelous heroine."
—Catherine Gilbert Murdock, author of
The Book of Boy and *Dairy Queen*

W9-COZ-641

OTHER BOOKS YOU MAY ENJOY

Ranger's Apprentice:
  The Ruins of Gorlan   John Flannagan

Three Times Lucky   Sheila Turnage

Roller Girl   Victoria Jamieson

The Inquisitor's Apprentice   Adam Gidwitz

The War that Saved My Life   Kimberly Brubaker Bradley

Ronia, the Robber's Daughter   Astrid Lindgren

The Forbidden Library   Django Wexler

A Tale Dark and Grimm   Adam Gidwitz

THE CLIFF

Drest stumbled back, back, nearly tripping on a loose clump of gorse.

"Crossbows!" bellowed Sir Oswyn.

She bolted down the nearest bank into the ravine. With a shower of pebbles and dirt in her wake, Drest reached the bottom and sprinted toward the cliff.

Someone shouted in the distance. Soil and stones crashed as castle men rushed into the ravine after her.

Drest wove between trees, focusing only on her speed and her direction, trying to remember where on the cliff the rope was waiting.

This was the most important race of her life.

Harkniss
Castle

Port with stable

The Ravine

Headland

sparse
woods

Juniper
Bush

Boggy
Ground

The Main Road

cliff with a stream

fallen Log

Phearsham
Ridge

Faintree
Castle

THE
LOWLANDS

Birrensgate

ⱽ.ⱽ.ⱽ = Drest's Path
━━━ = Main Road
• = Rest Stops

The Hunt for the MAD WOLF'S Daughter

—◇—

DIANE MAGRAS

PUFFIN BOOKS

To Benjamin and Michael,

my favorite castle men

⊰⊹⊱

PUFFIN BOOKS

An imprint of Penguin Random House LLC, New York

First published in the United States of America by Kathy Dawson Books
Published by Puffin Books, an imprint of Penguin Random House LLC, 2020

Visit us online at penguinrandomhouse.com

THE LIBRARY OF CONGRESS HAS CATALOGED THE KATHY DAWSON BOOKS EDITION AS FOLLOWS:
Names: Magras, Diane, author.
Title: The hunt for the Mad Wolf's daughter / Diane Magras.
Description: New York, NY : Kathy Dawson Books, [2019] | Summary: In 1210 Scotland,
twelve-year-old Drest is on the run with a price on her head after rescuing her brothers and
father, the Mad Wolf of the North, from captivity.
Identifiers: LCCN 2018034335 (print) | LCCN 2018040115 (ebook) |
ISBN 9780735229303 (E-book) | ISBN 9780735229297 (hardback)
Subjects: | CYAC: Adventure and adventurers—Fiction. | Heroes—Fiction. | Sex role—Fiction. |
Knights and knighthood—Fiction. | Middle Ages—Fiction. | Family life—Scotland—Fiction. |
Scotland—History—1057–1603—Fiction. | BISAC: JUVENILE FICTION / Action
& Adventure / General. | JUVENILE FICTION / Historical / Medieval. |
JUVENILE FICTION / Family / General (see also headings under Social Issues).
Classification: LCC PZ7.1.M34 (ebook) | LCC PZ7.1.M34 Hun 2019 (print) | DDC
[Fic]—dc23
LC record available at https://lccn.loc.gov/2018034335

Puffin Books ISBN 9780735229310

Map art by Sophie E. Tallis
Designed by Mina Chung • Text set in Dante MT

Printed in the United States of America

1 3 5 7 9 10 8 6 4 2

-◄- CONTENTS -►►-

Down the cracked stones did the young warrior crawl,
no blade at her hip, but her fury afire;
tearing chunks with her claws from the castle's wall,
whilst the sea at her heels surged higher;
aye, the great sea below surged higher.

In the castle rose knights, from foot and from knee,
and ran to the lord's chamber, swords drawn.
But all that they saw was the lass in the sea,
and the castle's young lord was gone—
aye, caught in her teeth, he was gone.

—*Anonymous*, AD *1210, Faintree Castle*

↞ 1 ↠

THE WARNING

A crow's shattering *creea* sounded beyond the healer's hut from somewhere on the village path.

"Did you hear that?" Drest bolted up from the floor, thumping her shoulder painfully against the heavy wooden bed. "That's Tig's crow."

"Was it one call?" Emerick, the injured knight—nay, *lord*—who had been her companion for the past six days, sat up and pushed away the blankets. "Or was that two? Drest, can you defeat two enemies?"

She reached up for the dagger sheathed against her ribs. "I can try."

"No, what am I saying? I'm half-asleep." He wiped his fair hair from his sweating forehead. "Will you help me up? We must hide in the woods." He tried to swing his legs over the bed, but stopped, seized in pain.

Carefully but firmly, Drest pushed him back onto the bed. "Nay, we don't need to hide. Mordag was only waking you, Emerick. She knows how well you heal when you're woken in the night and need to flee." She patted his bandaged chest. "This is nearly as good as being on the road, is it not?"

"I have my soundest sleep, of course, when I'm woken every few hours fearing for my life." He wet his lips. "*Was* that one call, or two? Where's Tig? Has he not heard Mordag's warning?"

"Tig's at the mill and he's surely heard it. But if you like, I'll go out and see what's there." Drest pointed to Wimarca, the village healer, who was sleeping by the circle of embers in the center of the room. "Wake her if you need her."

"*If* I need her? Drest, there is surely someone out there. Mordag doesn't make that call for nothing." Emerick grabbed her arm, his grip surprisingly strong, though it trembled. "You've not slept for I don't know *how* many days. You've barely eaten. If you try to challenge anyone, you'll fall. Drest, you're weak as a kitten—"

"A wolf cub. I'm as weak as a wolf cub who smells its prey." Gently, Drest pried his fingers from her arm. "And if I find someone, I'll slay him, or hide from him, or mock him. I'm good at that, see. And I'll be back before you know."

Emerick frowned. "If Mordag is warning us of knights again, you must run. Run where they cannot find you.

Wimarca can help *me*, but *you* must go, as swiftly as you can. If they catch you, they'll kill you this time."

Drest scrambled away from the bed, no longer in Emerick's reach. "Are you worried for me? Strange. I *am* a legend, and I seem to make it through anything that tries to set me back. I've saved your life twice. I intend to do it again."

"Thrice," Emerick said gloomily. "You've saved my life thrice." He sighed. "Please be careful."

"I always *am*."

She bowed low, then slipped to the door and outside.

⤛ 2 ⤜

THE TERROR OF THE WOODS

Drest trotted away from the hut and into the woods, her jeweled dagger now drawn. It made her feel strong, though a sword at her hip would have made her feel better. Once she was deep among the trees, she listened, then went on. She brushed past leafy branches, over mossy stones, as silent as the mist that shrouded the night around her.

Each time she'd heard Mordag's call for the past week, an enemy had been near:

A bandit on the dusty road.

A knight with his sword raised in a castle chamber.

An army of castle men streaming into the woods after her family.

The crow called again: a lingering note of warning. It was louder now, and close.

Drest shivered in her thin tunic with its ripped-off sleeves. The night was cold and damp. All around her, the trees formed monstrous shapes, their branches weaving above her head to block out the sky.

And there she was, sleep pulling at her consciousness like a stone in a net, alone in the woods.

Alone. Yet not alone: Her father and brothers were resting at the mill, ready to leap to their feet with their weapons.

But they didn't *have* their weapons, she remembered: All their swords had been broken or taken from them when they'd been captured at their headland home. Her family had hung from iron rings in Faintree Castle's prison for five days. The only weapons they would have would be the ones they'd stolen during their escape.

Nay, but our hands are our greatest weapons yet, said a rumbling deep voice in her mind: her eldest brother, Wulfric. She had long imagined her brothers' voices when she had been alone before. Wulfric's voice softened the edge from her fear.

Perhaps we've all heard Mordag as well, came her favorite brother Gobin's voice, a smile in his words. *You know what that means, do you not, lass?*

We'll be prowling, said his twin, Nutkin. *The terror of the woods.*

Drest shook her head. They had never been prowling in real life when she'd imagined their voices like that, which meant that she was still alone.

The best you can hope for is your lad Tig. The voice of Thorkill, her second-eldest brother, was thoughtful and

5

calm. *He's heard his crow, and he'll come out to see what she's calling about.*

The best you can hope for is to dig up your own courage wherever you've buried it, you mewing squirrel-brained fish-gut, sneered the voice of Uwen, her youngest brother.

Drest searched the trunks around her for the twins' black-haired phantom shapes, or the towering figures of Wulfric or Thorkill, or Uwen's smaller one.

But there was no sign of them.

Nor of Grimbol, her father, the Mad Wolf of the North—who would have ordered her to wait for the war-band and not go out alone.

I may be alone, but I'm not frightened, Drest thought. *I've seen my family captured by enemies, been under a bandit's knife, and hung from a ring in a dark and horrible prison. These are only woods.*

Another call from Mordag, harsh and desolate—from the other side of the village.

Near the mill.

Where all of Drest's family were sleeping.

Drest broke into a run, her pace long and swift, toward the faded echo of the call.

She emerged into the hay field at the top of the village, a sea of murky green in the dark. Stalks whispered beneath her feet as she skirted the edge.

Soon she was at the town square by the mill. That squat building with its wheel on the stream was but a deeper shadow in the night.

Silence. Not even wind.

Yet Mordag had called from the mill. The crow had never been wrong before. Something was surely out there.

Drest started to cross the dusty square, her eyes on the mill. Nothing was moving. The shadows were heavy.

Halfway there, Drest shot a glance down the grassy path that led to the villagers' huts.

She froze.

In the center of the path stood a knight. Even in the dark, his chain mail hood seemed to glimmer as he turned toward her.

⊸ 3 ⊷

THE WOLF'S HEAD

Terror pricked the back of Drest's neck. But a thrill as sharp as lightning branched throughout her too. She was there alone to battle a knight. And she was a legend, as Tig had always said.

Yet Emerick's warning flared in her mind.

The knight was advancing slowly, his chain mail hauberk clinking as he moved.

I'll make him chase me. His chain mail will slow him. And I'm faster than even the twins.

Drest darted back into the woods. In the corner of her eye, she could see the knight following. A dagger suddenly gleamed in his hand.

She slipped deeper among the trees, tearing past the branches, running so lightly her toes barely touched the soil.

The knight was close behind. Despite his armor, he didn't stumble, and didn't slow.

Suddenly he was at her heels, too close—

She was falling, sprawled across the branches and moss, one ankle caught by a hand.

Drest kicked wildly, but felt a hand around her other ankle too.

"Hold still," the knight snarled.

Drest lashed out at him with her dagger, but her blow only clanged against his armor.

"Ha! You'll try to fight me, will you?"

He knelt on her ankles, the chain mail on his knees scraping her skin through her hose, and grabbed her wrist. He squeezed hard, trying to make her drop her dagger.

Drest twisted her arm, shifted her dagger to her right hand, and lashed out again.

She was too quick for him to block, but the knight rolled off her, just missing her blow. He was on his feet as Drest scrambled up.

"I knew you'd be here," said the knight. "Yes, in the town that all the knights avoid. Where else would you go? You're Grimbol's son, and this is Grimbol's town, and here you are to do Grimbol's bidding. Have you put our poor lord's body in one of those village huts? Tell me where. You don't need it now that he's dead."

He thinks I've slain Emerick! Drest thought. *Why would he think that?* She almost began to speak, but Gobin's voice stopped her.

Or he's pretending he thinks that, and wants you to say where the lord is hiding. Take care, lass.

9

Drest retreated, holding her dagger between them. "Are you faithful to Lord Faintree?"

"*Am* I faithful? *Was* I faithful to the man you murdered, you mean. And the answer is yes: A knight is not a knight unless he's faithful. Now, did *you* slay him, or was it your father?"

She hesitated. "He's not dead. I was saving his life at the castle, not slaying him."

The knight smiled; his teeth showed in the darkness. "Then where is he? In this village?"

She backed away still farther. Something about his voice—and that smile—made her uneasy. "Nay, he's not in the village; my family's only passing by. If I tell you where he is, what will you do?"

"I'll tell his dear old uncle, a noble knight called Sir Oswyn. Yes, Sir Oswyn will be *very* glad to know where his nephew's hiding—"

His hand lashed out, grabbing, but it only grazed her cheek as she dove out of his reach.

"God's blood," whispered the man. "No one said you were a *lass*."

She barely heard him. She was running again, veering her path to lead him away from the village.

He grunted as he followed, his chain mail hauberk rattling. But the hauberk *was* heavy, and though he tried to keep up, he wasn't strong enough. He lagged. Soon Drest could no longer see him behind her. She started to look for a tree to climb.

It would be risky: If he saw her do it, he could wait below and she'd be trapped. But if she kept running and he caught up with her again, she might not be so lucky to escape a second time.

She turned to the nearest big tree: an ancient beech.

Drest scrambled up the trunk. Hand over hand, barely making a sound, she climbed until she reached a strong perch high above the other branches. Gripping that branch, she waited, panting with short sharp breaths through her nostrils alone—a trick she had taught herself when playing hiding games with Uwen.

"The *devil's* tail." The knight was below, circling a nearby oak. Through its interlacing branches, his figure was barely visible. "Where've you gone? You can't have disappeared."

Drest set her cheek against the trunk.

A scrape, followed by a loud crunch: The knight must have tripped on a downed branch.

"God's *blood!*"

Grumbling, he rose.

"Grimbol's youngest," he murmured, "and not a lad but a lass. And she knows where the lord's gone. Soggyweald, maybe? I'll have to look. If I find him, I'll tell Sir Oswyn.

What honor I'd gain from *that*. But her—that's thirty pounds if I catch that wolf's head first."

Drest closed her eyes. Her heart was thumping in her ears.

"Bah." Branches cracked as he stepped away from the trees. "You're gone. You're at the village, I warrant, rousing the rest of your brood." A pause. "What a wasted chance. I almost had you: a wolf's head who could give me back my honor, *and* give me thirty silver pounds. Yes, a proper wolf's head with *that* price."

He sniffed, then started back the way he'd come.

Drest waited until she heard his steps grow distant. She scrambled down.

What a bat-headed old man, said Uwen's voice. *Why don't you rush up after him and stick your dagger in his back? That would be a right surprise!*

But Drest didn't move. She stood at the base of the tree, rubbing her cold bare arms. The knight's words had lodged in her mind:

A wolf's head with that *price.*

◂◂ 4 ▸▸

SECRETS

As the village's grassy path came into sight between the trees, a black flash swept above—Mordag. The crow landed on a branch near Drest's head and twisted around to face her.

"*There* you are!" A pale boy with shaggy black hair, garbed in a filthy azure-blue tunic and black hose, ran up, panting. "I heard Mordag and rushed down to Wimarca's hut, but you'd already gone." He paused. "Yes, I know it's silly to think I might have helped you, but—well, I *thought* I might. Did you see anyone?"

"Aye, I saw a knight, Tig, thanks to your crow. He's gone now." Drest bit her lip. The knight's words were a shadow in her mind.

"Emerick said you went out to see who was there, but I didn't think you'd challenge anyone, not without your family." He faltered. "*Did* you challenge him alone?"

"Nay, I just led him off. Tig—he said I'm a wolf's head with a price." She shuddered. "What does that mean?"

"Did he tell you that?" Tig's face clouded. "I wouldn't think he'd say it to the person he's hunting."

A sick feeling passed through Drest. "Are they hunting me? What does it *mean,* Tig?"

"It means that you're akin to a wolf. And if anyone slays you, they—they get paid." Tig darted to her side. "I won't let them. I'll—Mordag and I will warn you each time an enemy comes near."

Drest crossed her arms. "I won't let them, either. It's just—" She broke off. "Where's Emerick?"

"He's gone to hide," Tig said distractedly. "The twins took him, and the rest of your brothers scattered looking for you, and—Drest, are you *sure* the knight called you a wolf's head?"

"Aye, I heard him, didn't I?" Her left hand brushed her right hip, where her sword should have hung. "Da's not going to be happy about this."

"No," Tig said, his voice rushed, "don't tell anyone. That price will be paid to whoever slays you, and if your family should mention it—that's the kind of thing that no one should say." Tig straightened his tunic. "I suppose that's what can happen when one becomes a legend."

Drest and Tig went in search of her brothers. Mordag led them, swooping over the trees. The crow circled near a cluster of gray-barked alders and gave a hoarse call—the call for a friend—above Uwen and Thorkill.

"I know Da says warriors must be up for *everything*," Uwen was grumbling, bent over, his hands on his knees, "but can a warrior not have a single night's rest after hanging for five days and nights from a ring in a cold, wet, dark, *stinking* prison?"

Thorkill reached down and patted the boy's back. "Aye, and we all thought those five days and nights were to be our last. You managed it well, lad. I heard nary a word from you all that time."

"I was ready to gripe as soon as they put us in there. I was even ready to cry. But Da would have shouted at me. So I hung there like a grub-headed squirrel."

Drest slipped through the trees. "That's because you *are* a grub-headed squirrel with a belly full of crabs."

Uwen straightened, then lunged for her. He closed his arms around her before she could twist away—and hugged her fiercely.

When had her teasing, taunting, whiny battle-mate ever hugged her like that? Then Drest remembered: When she'd rescued him from Faintree Castle's prison.

"What were you thinking, you rot-brained hare's bottom?" Uwen said. "Running off without telling anyone. You're part of a war-band. Have you forgotten the codes?

How can you shuttle your courage with someone you trust if no one's there, you midge?" Uwen sniffed and buried his face in her shoulder.

Thorkill tousled Drest's hair. "Ah, lass. All that time in the prison, we spoke of nothing but you: Had she escaped? Was she safe? Would she find what she needed to eat? And when we were all together, I thought, *We'll never leave her again*. But *you* left *us* tonight."

Drest struggled out of Uwen's grasp. "I had to. If I went back to the mill, the knight would have followed me there." She looked from Uwen to Thorkill. "I led him deep in the woods to give you time to wake and be ready."

She waited for them to praise her.

"Lass," Thorkill said, stroking his ginger beard, "we heard your lad's crow, so we were up and ready for battle— ready to fight one man. But we couldn't find him." His smile was sad. "He owes you his life."

Drest's jaw tightened. "Maybe he does, but I didn't see any of *you* outside when I needed you."

But she knew now what she should have done: led him directly to the mill. She should have trusted her brothers' years of training.

"I'm sorry," Drest muttered, her throat thick.

"We'll catch him next time," Thorkill said. "Nay, lass,

there's no reason to brood when you can learn from your mistake and no one's been hurt."

Uwen slung an arm around her shoulders. "*I* wasn't ready. And Wulfric's the only one with a sword. Thorkill, would you have had time to slot an arrow in your bow with a man rushing at you? He'd probably have slain me while you struggled with the string. *I* owe *you* my life, Drest." The lad leaned toward his sister and gave her a noisy kiss on her cheek.

"That knight," Drest said. "He—"

As she drew out the words, Tig clicked his tongue, interrupting. With a long *caa*, Mordag landed on his out-stretched arm.

Why can't I tell them? Drest tried to ask the question with her eyes, but Tig wasn't looking at her.

"What were you saying of that knight?" Thorkill prompted.

She met her brother's gentle brown eyes. "I'm sorry I didn't slay him when I had the chance."

She'd keep the secret. For now.

GRIMBOL'S ORDERS

By dawn, Drest's family was together in the healer's hut, a place where they could talk by themselves while Emerick was being tended. The young lord lay in bed. Wimarca bent over him, applying fresh salve and bandages to replace the ones that had been dislodged by his flight. The room was rich with the scent of herbs: biting and clean, almost like the sea.

Grimbol was conferring with each of his sons. Drest had seen him do that after battles when the war-band had come home and her brothers were sitting around the bonfire, their meat and ale in hand. Grimbol would tell them where they had lapsed and what they could do better, and though his voice had always been gentle, it had seemed like a blade at the end. He was talking to the lads in order of their ages—Wulfric, then Thorkill, Gobin and Nutkin, then Uwen. He was speaking with Uwen now, and the lad was rubbing his nose.

Drest was leaning against the wall, apart from everyone, itching to tell Gobin her secret. Her favorite brother and his twin were directly across from her, their silky black hair stark against their pale faces. She had always told Gobin her secrets, though none before had really mattered.

She stiffened: Grimbol was watching her.

He ambled over to her side. "I'm proud of you, lass," he said in his low, rough voice, "for all you've done, and how you've proved yourself. You've been everything I could've expected of you—nay, far more."

The fire crackled behind them.

"But next time," Grimbol went on, a flicker of iron in his words, "*I* make the plans, not you. Come to me when you need to make a choice, and I shall give you an order to obey, for that's the way of a war-band."

The Mad Wolf of the North kissed his daughter's forehead with a touch as gentle as a flower. He turned back to his sons.

The last order you gave me was to be like the barnacle and hie to the eagle's roost, Drest thought. *None of you would be here now if I'd obeyed.* But she said nothing.

"That knight was a scout," said Grimbol. "I know the castle's ways: Oswyn sent him to find us, and that knight will have a war-band on his heels when he comes back. We haven't the weapons to fight a castle war-band and win. Not this time. We'll bide here until night, then go, and keep going from every place. This will be our life until the hunt for us slows."

Uwen slumped.

Grimbol patted his son's shoulder as he walked past him to the bed where Emerick was sitting up with Wimarca's help. "Lord, I'm sorry, but your uncle is hunting you too, so you'll need to come with us. But do not fear: He'll not catch us as long as we do not tarry. You're mended now?"

"I would not call it that," said Wimarca. "A man cannot be sewn like a cloth and made as good as new."

"Aye, but he can be mended enough to move." Grimbol gestured to the floor. "Stand for me, lord."

Wimarca pulled the tunic down over Emerick's bandages. "No, he shall not stand for you. He shall take my advice and lie back upon that bed and heal."

Grimbol's eyes narrowed. "I cannot leave our lord here to be plucked and murdered like a bird from its nest. Be out of my way, old woman, before you make me angry."

Drest held her breath. Her father's code of life and war included the rule to honor all matrons and maidens. *This* was not honor.

"Be wary of making *me* angry," Wimarca snapped. "Grimbol, you've no choice. He must have five days more to heal. *Five.* Then you may take him where you like. But not until then."

Grimbol's hard, cold eyes softened. "Your salves are powerful, though. He may heal faster than you think."

His face set in thought, he walked to the center of the room.

"We'll be sitting birds in the nest ourselves if we stay," he murmured. Then he shook his head. "Nay, a village should be able to protect its lord. I've protected this lazy village for many years, and asked for no payment. I shall ask for it now."

Grimbol pointed at Tig, who had been watching everything from behind the fire.

"Tell your foster father I want a word with him," said the old warrior. "Tell him to wait for me in the mill. I'll be up soon."

"I'm not sure he'll want a word with *you*," Tig muttered under his breath. But he rose and darted out of the hut.

Grimbol and Arnulf the miller stood facing each other in the mill's big room, their families at their backs like two sides in a battle. Drest's brothers stood according to their ages, a line of fierce warriors even without their weapons. Wyneck, the miller's son and Tig's foster brother, stood behind his father, his fingers in his beard. His fair-haired sister, Idony, was frowning at his side with Tig. Grimbol had also summoned Torold the blacksmith on his way to the mill. That broad-shouldered man stood next to the miller, staring uneasily at the war-band.

Drest stood far enough from each group to be part of neither. After a few moments, Tig slipped away from his sister and went to Drest. They exchanged quick smiles, then Drest rocked back on her heels in her most arrogant warrior pose, one like Wulfric's: knees slightly bent, arms crossed, chin high.

"Arnulf, my daughter tells me you call this *my* village," Grimbol said, his rough voice filling the cavernous room.

"Yes, sir, it is. Your war-band has protected us over the years. And we are grateful." Arnulf frowned. "Have we not served you well this night, sir? Do your sons and lass want other beds? And—his lordship—"

"Aye, you've served me well this night, but this whole village owes me more than that. I want my dues for those years of protection."

Arnulf paled. "We have neither coin nor wheat—"

"Your dues are your village men. There's a traitor leading Faintree Castle who's hunting my lord and me. My lads and I are leaving before he finds us, but Lord Faintree is still too wounded to flee. Your village men will guard him while he heals."

Tig's foster family exchanged looks.

"Guard?" murmured Arnulf. "We are not warriors, sir."

"All you'll do is stand watch in the woods and take the lord to safety if you see a castle man. And aye, you'll need

22

to fight for his life if it comes to that, but it won't if you do the rest well. I'll be back in five days, when the lord's healed enough to travel, and take him then. But for those five days, every man of this village must do my bidding."

"How can you ask that?" breathed Idony. "If you and your lads cannot stand against a war-band of castle men, how will our village men? They don't know how to guard *or* fight!"

"They'll *learn*," growled the Mad Wolf. "Arnulf, tell the farmers to come hear my orders. Gather them before midday."

"Sir, the farmers must tend the wheat and barley—"

"The fields can wait." Grimbol pointed at Wyneck. "You. I want you to lead this watch."

The miller's son shook his head. "I don't know how to watch or guard against castle men, sir. Idony's right; none of us do."

Grimbol broke from the line of his family. He seemed about to cross the line of villagers and head for the door, but he stopped: inches away from Wyneck. The younger man was taller than him by a hand, but still Wyneck flinched.

"You *will* lead the watch," said Grimbol, his voice soft and menacing. "You and your men will be strong by your numbers. You will use those numbers to protect Lord Faintree. If I return and find my lord harmed, I shall burn your village to the ground—and every one of you along with it."

Drest shrank. This was not the father she knew, the man who had tucked her beneath his arm by the bonfire on the headland, the da who had told her stories. This was the villain from all the tales that Emerick had told her of her father.

Grimbol turned to Idony.

"You: Fetch enough food for my family for five days. Have it ready by dusk." He pivoted to face Torold the blacksmith. "You: I need swords for all my sons and daughter."

Torold shook his head. "I have not the steel."

"Find it."

Grimbol returned to his sons. "Someone has to keep watch in the woods for castle men before we leave tonight. You're tired, lads, but which of you will take this on?"

The war-band hesitated.

"I will," said Drest. "Where should I go? All the woods around?"

In truth, she wanted to be away from her family, to be alone in the woods, and to run. Her limbs were aching to move.

But Grimbol shook his head. "Nay, lass, not you."

The twins stepped forward.

"Da, Nutkin and I will keep watch," Gobin said. "Drest, you should get some sleep."

"You've done your work already," added Nutkin.

"Aye, my wee sister, you've spent half the night in the woods," rumbled Wulfric.

"But there she goes, offering to keep watch, though she's been on her feet and on the road longer than the rest of us," Thorkill said. "My poor wee lass, you must be ready to drop."

"Nay, not unless it's to drop a giant stone on someone's head," Uwen said cheerfully.

They were all smiling at her. But the knot in her stomach remained.

Torold the blacksmith began to back away. Grimbol swung around to face him, his hand at his dagger.

"Where are you going?" he snapped.

"I was going to our healer when you fetched me, sir. My wee brother is injured, like the lord, and needs Wimarca's salve."

Drest looked down. She had nearly slain Colum, Torold's wee brother, in a battle to defend Tig when she had first come to the village.

"Do what you will," growled the old warrior, "but bring me the weapons I asked for by tonight."

Torold hesitated. "Sir, I have no steel. And I cannot smelt

steel as quickly as you wish. It will take me more than a day to smelt even enough for a dagger."

"No steel? What did you use, then, for the blade-edge of the axe I saw in your smithy? You can take its steel for us." Grimbol nodded at Wulfric. "Go with him. See what steel he has. Thorkill and Uwen, help Arnulf gather our village men. And Drest—go back to your lord."

Drest wanted to tell her father to leave the villagers alone. But a small voice warned her not to confront him in front of everyone.

The voice also whispered, *You've just seen it come to life: Grimbol's legend.*

6

THE PRICE

Back in Wimarca's hut, Emerick sat stiff and pale. The healer had gone out to gather plants and bark from the woods, and Drest and Tig were alone with him.

"Your father has just oppressed my villagers." Emerick was breathing hard. "I vowed I would never be cruel like my own father, and look—Grimbol's taken my authority and struts like a lordly brute. The villagers will think I gave my power to him, that I'm a submissive member of his war-band. I said I wouldn't join it, but everyone will think I did."

"They'll think you're a helpless *victim* of his war-band, if that makes you feel better," said Tig.

"No, that doesn't make me feel better." Emerick's voice was harsh. "God's breath. The farmers need to tend their crops; this is a crucial time for the fields. And they are not warriors. What is he thinking? Forcing them to do what they cannot do easily or well will only anger them. And what will *I* do with a mob of resentful villagers?" Emerick held his breath, his face stiff with pain.

Tig knelt by the fire and filled a wooden cup from the pot. He carried it to Emerick's bed and pressed it into his hands. "This is a caudle. It may smell like poison, taste like poison, and burn like poison, but I promise it's *still* a caudle."

Emerick drank, and winced. "It tastes worse than poison."

"Swallow it quick."

Emerick did, then held the cup back. "This works far better than the caudles they make at the castle, though: My stomach is already numb. I wish I could say that for the rest of me." He let out a sigh, and gave Drest a grim smile. "I'm sorry. I should have told you to wake your family last night. I didn't care to see Grimbol scold you like that."

Drest eased herself away from the wall. She had forgotten her father's scolding. Her stomach was in knots from something else. "Emerick, what it does mean if a knight puts a price on your head?"

Tig frowned.

"That's sweet of you, Drest, but I don't think my uncle Oswyn has put a price on my head; I'm sure he's just promised a new privilege—like instant knighthood—to anyone who slays me. It's not about money." He paused. "That's not what you meant. What *did* you mean? Tig, why are you squirming?"

"I'm twitching, not squirming."

Drest twisted her fingers together. "Tig said I can't tell anyone, but—"

"And there's a very good reason for that!" Tig groaned. "The more people who know, the more likely it is that someone will mention it by mistake!"

"God's bones," cried Emerick. "There's a price on *Drest's* head? Where did you learn this?"

"The knight who was chasing me. He said there's a price on my—my wolf's head."

A dark look came into Emerick's face. "*That* is not legal. Women cannot have *that* on their heads, and—God's blood, you're *twelve*. It's only for men *far* older than you."

Drest bit her lip. "The knight said he'd get thirty silver pounds for me."

Emerick scowled. "I'll strip that knave of his knighthood, have him whipped, then strung up like a hen before a feast—as soon as I get back to the castle." He patted the side of his bed. "Come, Drest, let's talk about this. It's right that you told me. I've dealt with this sort of thing before."

In two long strides, Drest was at the bed. She plopped beside him.

Gingerly, careful of his rib wound, he reached over and squeezed her shoulder. "A wolf's head means that anyone—child, farmer, bandit, or knight—will be paid if they bring my uncle Oswyn your head. It's not something my father ever did. He preferred to imprison his enemies and let them slowly die on their rings above the sea. Oswyn was following that tradition with your family—no one has ever escaped our prison before, and your family wasn't going anywhere until you came—but you, my friend, escaped in less than a day. So you're more dangerous than your father. Which is why he's passed this sentence on you alone."

"Does Oswyn know that she's protecting you?" Tig said.

"He knows I'm alive and he saw Drest at the castle, so yes, he surely understands that now." He frowned. "No doubt he's *told* everyone that she's kidnapped and murdered me, though. Oh Drest, with this sentence on your head, even my *loyal* men will slay you."

"How can he tell them I've slain you?" Drest grumbled. "Did he not see me in the window with you? Is it not obvious that I rescued you? How is it so easy for your uncle to lie?"

"Drest, it's more than an easy lie; it's what appears to be the truth. Yes, he saw you in the window, but he didn't see us together. They must have found Sir Maldred's body on the rocks below and surmised that you slew him. Everyone knows that you must have freed your family; they'd been trapped for all those days until you came. Then you escaped from the castle without anyone seeing you, and now I'm missing." He gave Drest a faded smile.

"I expect you've become quite the legend at my castle."

The thatch above their head creaked in the wind, and a stray piece of straw drifted down. It wavered, then sank beside the pot into the fire, and instantly flared.

Emerick lay back upon the pillow. "Drest, I'm sorry. This should not be your reward for saving my life. I wish I could stop it."

"You can," said Tig, "if you mention this to no one. Drest, you too."

"Aye, you keep saying that. But why shouldn't I tell my family?"

"Words travel," Tig said darkly. "Since they love you, Drest, they'll speak of it, and plot, and plan. And each time they do, someone else might hear. I know how this works."

"Don't tell me someone once put a price on *your* head," Emerick murmured.

Tig crossed the room to the pot and knelt beside it. "How do you think everyone here knows that my mother was a witch? *I* didn't tell. Except Idony, once. And then she told Wyneck, who told Arnulf, and someone overheard. The other villagers began to talk about making Arnulf turn me out of this village. I was too dangerous to keep, you see."

"You were but six years old when you first came here, were you not?" Drest asked. "And they spoke of turning you out? Tell me who."

31

"No, I won't tell you who. But yes, it *was* cruel. Which is why Wimarca mentioned to a farmer one day that she was glad they'd taken me in, for that meant that my witch mother's spirit would make the harvest rich. It really *wasn't* very rich that year, but everyone believed that what *had* grown was because of my poor mother." He glanced up. "So let's feed no rumors, please. This has to be our secret."

Emerick sighed. "But my uncle will do everything in his power to spread the word."

"Not in *this* village." Tig gave a bitter laugh. "Remember, Emerick, Phearsham Ridge is no friend to Faintree Castle. Everyone knows that the castle men who come here rarely leave."

Uneasily, Drest watched them talk. The villagers might hate Faintree Castle, but they would hate Grimbol even more for enlisting their men against their will.

⊰ 7 ⊱

A LORD'S ORDERS

"I don't know why we have to go *tonight*," Uwen whined, kicking a pale pink blossom from its stem. "I want to sleep."

Uwen, Drest, Thorkill, and the twins were gathered outside Wimarca's hut, waiting for their father's order. It was almost dusk, and their last order had been to rest but be ready to leave at a moment's notice.

"Uwen, lad, you know it's not safe for us here," sighed Thorkill. He was on his knees in the grass, carving the bark off sticks and giving them sharp points: simple arrows for his bow. Emerick was leaning against the doorway behind him, swathed in a trailing blanket.

"I say we go up to the huts and take whatever beds we want and slay the villagers who try to stop us." With a swift kick, Uwen sent a heavy purple blossom tumbling.

"I say we put your head in the healer's pot," muttered Gobin, "and let her turn it into stew. A great deal of good *your* mind is doing us."

Thorkill sighed again and began to carve another stick.

Drest nodded at her youngest brother. "Why don't you sleep in Emerick's bed? He's not in it now."

"*You* sleep in it, you lazy feathered slug."

"Insult her again," snarled Gobin, "and I'll break your face."

"And *I'll* break the back of your neck," added Nutkin.

Uwen reddened. "I'll break *you*, you boar-witted toads! I'll break your heads together!"

Thorkill slammed down a half-sharpened stick. "If I hear one more word from *any* of you, I shall take him to the river and dunk him until I've drowned sense into him. This unraveling of control makes men fail on a battle-field—"

"But we're *not* on a battlefield!" Uwen burst out. "We're in a stinking village in a filthy hut, and we're about to go traveling for *days* and—"

"Look, you've done it now," crowed Gobin.

In seconds, Thorkill had Uwen's shoulder in one hand and Gobin's in the other. "I warned you both. So it's time for a bath, lads."

Drest ran to Thorkill's side. Both Uwen and Gobin were struggling in his grip, but neither was any closer to getting free.

"There's an easy way to solve this," Drest said. "Let me

strike Uwen once. Then we'll be even, and we can all rest and—"

"I'll strike you so hard you'll want to go hide in a *real* maiden's shift!" howled Uwen.

"*Stop* it!"

The voice—sharp and low, fierce and noble—came from the door.

All the Mad Wolf's children froze.

Emerick was gripping the frame to keep upright, the blanket now pooled at his feet. But even though he stood there in his torn, dirty tunic with bare legs, there was majesty in his figure, and power too.

"We cannot have this. Every one of our lives is in danger."

Thorkill dropped his grip on his brothers. None of the four moved.

"Uwen." Emerick pointed to the boy. "Go sit by that white shrub. *Don't* kick it. And don't speak like that to Drest again. She's the only one of you who's had the courage to meet the enemy alone."

Uwen shuffled quickly to the white bush and sank to his knees.

"Gobin and Nutkin," Emerick went on in that hard, cold voice, "go over to those trees in the opposite corner. Sit quietly."

35

As if in one body, the twins silently retreated and settled onto the ground.

Thorkill let out a long laugh and went back to his weapons on the grass. "Well done, lord."

Emerick's mouth twitched. "Thank you."

Drest drifted to his side. "That was a fearsome voice."

"Ha. I can't keep *that* up for long. It's what my father called 'the *lord's* voice.' My sister, Celestria, was brilliant at it. I never could do it as well as she."

"Nay, lord, you did it well," said Uwen from his knees. "I was so scared I nearly wet my hose."

"It's a fine voice," Gobin called over his shoulder, "like your own battle cry."

"You really *are* all exceptionally trained," said Emerick. "Better than knights."

The twins twisted around, smiling. Thorkill grinned. Uwen beamed.

And even Drest felt warm: Only a week ago, Emerick had been telling her how much her family deserved to hang.

A black whir shot through the sky above them, circled, and Mordag landed in the thatch.

Tig came striding down the path. "Your father wants you now. And Emerick, he wants you as well, but only if you can walk."

"To the mill?" Emerick's hand tightened on Drest's shoulder. "I made it to the castle like this. Let's see what I can do."

It was dusk. Grimbol and Wulfric were kneeling on the grass by the mill, looking over the sacks of food that had been set there for their journey. As the rest of the war-band drew near, Emerick leaning on Drest, Grimbol stood and dusted off his knees.

"What do you think, lord? Are you feeling young and strong? You've walked all this way from the healer's hut. Have you rested enough to walk farther?"

Emerick was pale. "I doubt it. My ribs—the wound from Maldred's sword—"

"Nay, lord, if you're feeling it after that short walk, you cannot come with us. That's what I was afraid of." Grimbol sighed. "I don't like leaving you here alone. I do not trust the villagers to obey me when I am gone. Aye, one of us will have to stay behind."

"I want to stay," said Uwen. "Leave me, Da, and I'll protect the lord."

Drest scowled. "You only say that because you want to sleep. As soon as Da leaves, you'll curl upon the floor with a blanket and let anyone with a blade walk in. Nay, Da, leave me. I've protected Emerick before. And I'm friends with Arnulf and Wimarca and I can make friends with the other villagers—and I'll be safest here."

She waited, her heart pounding.

"Nay, lass," murmured her father. "We've been parted too much of late; I want you with me this time. Lads, which one of you will it be? Not Uwen, but of the rest?"

Silence but for the river's gurgling and the creaking of the mill wheel.

"Should you not ask *me* who should stay?" Emerick said slowly. "I want Drest." He paused. "And *that* is my order."

Grimbol slipped free his dagger, examined the blade, and tested it against his thumbnail. Then he sheathed it. His lips were twitching.

"You sound so much like your sister, lord, like my wee lady Celestria." Grimbol's voice was strangely light. "Is Drest who you really want, out of all of us?"

"Yes. She's saved my life enough times that I will not feel safe without her by my side. And she can protect herself as well. You can trust her, Grimbol."

The old warrior gestured for his daughter to come near. "Don't take risks, lass. If you see any castle men, call the village guards to take the lord into the fields and pretend he's a farmer. Draw off the castle men. Use your skills to lose them in the woods. Then go back and take the lord to the woods, and hide until they're gone. No fights, just running and hiding. Understand?" He turned to his sons. "Everyone, put a sack on your shoulder."

Drest skipped back to Emerick and ducked under his arm.

"Thank you," she whispered.

It was dark with a faint glimmer of the moon when the war-band reached the edge of the village laden with their supplies. Emerick had gone back to Wimarca's hut, and Drest was with them alone. Each of her brothers embraced her. A lump came to her throat as she hugged them back.

"Remember: If you're attacked, duck and parry," said Gobin.

"And make sure you have a stick," chimed in Nutkin. "Blast. We should have made her a spear."

"Our wee Drest can make her own spear," came Thorkill's gentle voice. "But make sure you run before you fight; I don't want to come back and find you hurt, lass."

Wulfric leaned down and kissed her cheek, his corded beard brushing against her. "Just be yourself, Drest, and all will be well."

"I wish I could stay with you, you bladder-headed squirrel's bottom," muttered Uwen in a choked voice.

Grimbol snapped his fingers. "Hunt formation, lads."

The twins slipped to the front of the group. Thorkill swung the longbow from his back as Uwen charged to his side, and Wulfric marched between the two pairs.

Grimbol nodded at Drest. "Take good care of our lord. And yourself. We'll be back in five days, maybe sooner."

Was his jaw trembling? She didn't have a good look; her father joined the lads at the end of their formation, and soon they were in the woods and, in moments, they were gone.

Drest waited until she could no longer hear their footsteps. Then she pivoted and headed back to the healer's hut.

↢ 8 ↣

THE VILLAGERS

Emerick was snoring, thanks to Wimarca's most recent sleeping draught. The old healer sat on her stool by the fire.

"I'm glad you are here, child," Wimarca said. "Tig tells me I have a legend in my hut. But do you know what pleases me most? Not that you are a legend, but that you are a friend—to Tig. That lad has not many friends in this village."

"I don't know why no one's been good to him," Drest said. "He's one of my greatest friends in all the world." She paused. "But *you've* been good. He told me how you protected him when he first came to this village."

"A witch's son inspires fear by his very presence. He cannot help it, and small-minded people cannot help their reactions. But it is not easy being different, and Tig is *very* different from other lads."

"Is it not a fine thing to be different from what people expect of you?" Drest shrugged.

Wimarca's old face creased in a smile. "It is good for this village to see that one such as you calls Tig your friend."

The healer stood and wandered to a large wooden chest, in the corner of her hut. There she knelt, opened the lid, and began to sort past weavings and linens and parchment tied with string. Then she removed a long sword-belt, worn with age and use, but oiled so that the leather shone. Beside it, Wimarca placed a long leather sheath covered with intricate whirls. When she took away her hand, Drest saw a hilt.

"Is that really a sword?" Drest murmured, unable to take her eyes from the plain square pommel, nicked and worn with battle, above the leather-wrapped grip. "Where did you get it?"

"From a fallen castle man. Yes, in the days long past when your father defended this village. I don't know what fancy made me take this weapon, but I did, and have kept it to call to me when its time was right. And its time is now, and its place is at your hip."

The belt was soft in Drest's hands, the leather a quality she had never touched before. She strapped it over her hips and slipped the scabbard with its sword into the loops. The sudden familiar weight against her leg made her chest lighten.

Drest drew the sword. It was large and heavy, a sword for a fighting man, like her last sword Borawyn had been. "Has it a name?"

42

"It may have had one in its distant past, but let me name it now as Tig would: Call this sword Tancored. Do you know who that is?"

Drest shook her head.

"Tancored is a fae in one of the Seelie legends of these parts. She teaches heroes to be their true selves."

Drest slipped the sword back into its scabbard. *Tancored.* That name felt right.

It was completely dark as Drest drifted into the woods. The farmers were stationed around the hut and on the path, and it was time for her to speak to them and show them that she was their friend and not just her father's daughter.

Still, she was nervous; she had spoken to few villagers but Tig's family, and was not entirely sure how she should address the others. Gruffly, repeating Grimbol's orders? Thanking them for their willingness to serve? Neither seemed natural.

Drest drew up to the spot by a cluster of rowan bushes where her father had set the nearest guard. But the bearded farmer whom Grimbol had put in place was no longer there. Had he taken a break? She stayed for a few minutes, listening, then walked on soundlessly to the second spot: a place by a stone near the path.

It too was empty.

Frowning, Drest darted on to the third spot, then the fourth. No villagers were guarding as they had been when Grimbol had left. There were none in the woods, nor on the path, nor in the fields.

Scowling now, Drest ran up toward the mill, past the stream, which was silent in the night, its sluice closed. She hoped that Arnulf would remember all she had done for Tig and see her as his foster son's friend and not as Grimbol's child, for she would have to rely on his word to make the farmers obey.

If they would listen to him.

Drest slipped up to the mill's back door, the one she had entered when she had first come to Phearsham Ridge, but hesitated. There was shouting inside, a booming noise, and not just from a handful of men.

I thought you said they were your friends, sneered Uwen's voice.

Drest crept in and put her hand on the door leading into the big room. Careful not to make a sound, she pushed open the door a crack—and stopped.

A mob of villagers and a roar of voices filled the room. Men, women, young and old, crowded within.

Drest caught her breath. It was like the mob in Soggyweald that had come to watch the witch Merewen burn.

"Quiet!" Arnulf's word cut through the noise.

The voices subsided into rumbling.

"I don't like having the lord here either," Arnulf said. "And no, we're not fit to guard him. But if we refuse, we'll have Grimbol's wrath to bear."

"Why not send his lord to another village?" The young bearded farmer whom Grimbol had placed in the spot by the rowan bushes raised his hand. "Send him to Soggy-weald and make him *their* problem."

The woman beside him—small, with a long dark braid and a dark-haired child in her arms—elbowed his ribs. "That's a fool's notion, Hodge. Refuse the Mad Wolf of the North? You might as well battle fire with your hands."

A chorus of women's voices agreed.

"Or give him back to the castle!" called another voice. "We'd be rewarded for that, surely."

"We'd be slaughtered for that!"

"I think it's all a lie," Hodge called. "Who says that the castle wants to kill its own lord? Grimbol, that's who. Because he wants *us* to risk *our* lives holding that sniveling, sorry lord hostage for him!"

More voices—men and women together—were chorusing their agreement. The noise was rising into a mindless pitch.

"You don't know the truth of it!"

The new voice cut through the rest: Torold. Drest saw

him through the crack. A wan boy swathed in bandages leaned against him: his brother Colum.

"I spoke to Lord Faintree," the blacksmith roared, "and this is what he said: Every one of Grimbol's words is true. His uncle wants the lord dead so he can have the castle for himself, and if we want—"

"So let his uncle have him!" an old woman interrupted.

"Is Grimbol going to order us to gain back the lord's castle for him?" shouted a man.

"He'd better not!" cried Hodge. "You may die for your lord if that's your wish, Torold, but *I'm* not fighting for him, nor for the Mad Wolf!"

"And why do *you* obey Grimbol's whim, Torold, when his wee beast of a lass did *that* to your brother?" called someone else.

Drest backed away from the door. Her hand closed over the square pommel of her new sword.

"I obey Lord Faintree, not the Mad Wolf!" bellowed Torold. "I know and honor the man who rules us! My lord says that Grimbol's lass is his guard—"

"And our curse!"

Someone laughed.

"You wouldn't laugh if you'd ever seen her fight!" shouted a thin, sharp voice: Tig's. "Do you have any idea

46

how many times she's saved *everyone's* life—including all of yours?"

"I say we grab the Wolf's lass *and* her rotten lord and bury them in the midden! Who's with me?" Hodge's voice rang out.

Another loud roar, the voices joining.

Drest retreated into the night.

The villagers were like wasps in a nest that had been struck: angry, unthinking, and dangerous.

What could she do? She would have to take Emerick into the woods and hide, constantly moving, as if she were her father.

But Emerick was not well enough to flee.

Drest shook her head. She would have to face the villagers. She had done so at Soggyweald, alone, only now Tig was on her side, and Torold too, somehow. And Arnulf, she was sure, would object to anyone who sought to harm her, and Wyneck and Idony would do the same. She'd have to find a way to win over the rest.

Or you could slay them, as Da would, said Gobin's casual voice.

Drest crept back inside the small room. The roar of the crowd was down to a murmur.

She put her eye to the crack—

—and saw the door on the other end of the room open. A tall figure in a dark brown cloak and hood slipped in.

"I beg your pardon," said the man in a pleasant, gentle voice. "Have I interrupted something?"

Drest's brow furrowed. The voice was familiar. She tried to think back to the people she'd met in her journey before but could not place him.

"I've stopped by, if I may, for a bite to eat. And to ask how safe is the road ahead. There are rumors everywhere about the Mad Wolf."

Drest knew that voice now.

It was the knight who had chased her, the one who'd spoken about the price on her head.

A TRAITOR

"You sound like a castle man." Arnulf's voice was cold and echoed in the mill's large room. "Who are you?"

"I'm Swithun the tanner of Brill's Gate. I *was* a castle man for many years. I was taken from my village to work at Faintree Castle at my trade. But I'm going home now; my term with them is up."

Liar, Drest thought. *I saw you wearing chain mail.*

A wee bairn began to cry.

"It's been a long time since we've seen a castle man in this village," Arnulf said slowly. "A *very* long time."

"Yes, I've heard it's not safe for castle men here. But I hoped that *I* might be welcome, just for a meal, being but a tanner." He paused. "Do you wish me to go?"

"Before you do," called another voice—Hodge's, Drest recognized—"I'd like to hear news. We've heard some rumors, see, about the Mad Wolf, and your Lord Faintree. Where's your lord gone? Do you know?"

Now the whole room was silent, but for the bairn's stuttering sobs.

Drest held her breath.

"He's not here, then?" said the man.

"No," said Hodge, "I wouldn't be asking you that if he were."

The man cleared his throat. "Where our young lord is: *That's* the question. One rumor says that when the Mad Wolf escaped from the castle prison, he caught the lord in his chamber, broke his neck, and threw him to the sea. But Sir Oswyn—he's our lord now—said he saw Grimbol's youngest—the bloodthirsty lass—in the young lord's chamber. He says she took him away and murdered him in a place sacred to her family. But not here, you say. So he must be somewhere else."

A low murmur crossed the room as the bairn's sobs became wails.

"I should mention," the man went on, "there's a price on her head. Three silver pounds. If any one of you should find her, tell me, and I'll be sure you get that."

Drest stumbled out onto the grass. Now all the villagers knew. Three silver pounds would be a fortune to anyone in Phearsham Ridge. And once he had her, the knight would be able to get the rest.

The door behind her flung open, and a small figure came

through, carrying the wailing baby. It was the woman with
the long black braid. At the sight of Drest, she gasped.

It would take only a moment for the woman to call back
to the mill, only a moment to earn her three silver pounds.

Drest's hand slipped down to her sword. For the first
time, her fingers shook as they closed around the grip.

"Hurry and come," said the woman, glancing back at
the door. "My name is Elys, and you can trust me. Quick,
before anyone else sees you."

And before Drest knew what was happening, Elys seized
her wrist and broke into a run along the path.

Drest sprinted alongside her, down to the cluster of
wattle-and-daub huts. They ducked inside the third in a
row, into darkness and the reeking scent of earth.

Elys let her daughter onto the packed dirt floor and
dragged the wooden door shut. "I can only imagine what
your life has been. But when Tig says a person is a friend, I
believe him."

A tiny bloom of relief washed over Drest. "That man.
He's not a tanner. He's the knight I saw early this morn."

Elys's dark eyes grew wide. "Are you sure?"

"Aye, he spoke to me. He—he said there's a mighty price
on my head, but I'm also a wolf's head, and he—" Drest
put her hand over her mouth.

"My *God*," murmured the woman.

51

She was at Drest's side, her arms around the girl, holding her tight.

"I'll not let him touch you. This is *not* a life a lass should lead—nay, not *any* child! I'll not let that filthy, lying rogue near you!"

Drest leaned into her embrace, forgetting for a moment everything but the feel of those strong arms around her, the powerful hand rubbing her back.

What about your lord, Drest? Wulfric's voice urged. *He's all alone, unprotected, in that hut.*

She pulled away. "That knight—I'm not safe while he's here, and I can't leave Emerick and—we can't stay in this village."

"We'd best get you both out before he finds you. Your lord—he needs clothes, does he not?" Elys grabbed a tunic and a pair of boots that were hanging from a rope on the wall. "Take Barbary. Pick her up under her arms."

Drest looked down. The bairn was sticking a fistful of rushes in her mouth.

"Quick! Before my Hodge comes back and sees you. Ah, that fool man with his mouth that never stops!"

Drest dropped to her knees and drew the bairn into her lap, then up into her arms.

"I won't hurt you," Drest promised, trying to be gentle as she lifted the wriggling, grumbling child.

Elys opened the door a crack, then sprang out. Drest caught up in seconds, and they ran together down the path, keeping to the shadows. Elys took a shortcut between the trees to the healer's hut. Mordag let out a welcoming *caa* from the roof.

Drest barreled inside after Elys.

"There you are!" cried Tig. "Thank goodness! There was a man at the mill, talking of the price—"

"I was there. Tig, that man was the knight who'd chased me!"

Wimarca shut the door behind them and took Barbary from Drest's arms.

Elys dropped her pile of clothing on the bed. "I'll help you dress, lord."

Mordag's harsh *creea* from outside seemed to shatter the air around them.

Tig rushed to Drest. "He's come! Quickly, hide!"

Barbary let out a ringing cry.

Drest looked around. The hut was small, with no room under the bed. The walls were bare and there was nothing that could conceal her.

Her hand closed over Tancored's grip, then slid up into her tunic to her dagger. She would have to attack the knight as he entered, and do it perfectly the first time.

"Can you climb the post?" Tig pointed to a support on

53

the side of the hut. "There's not much room in the thatch, but—"

Another barking call from Mordag, more urgent than the last.

Elys threw the blankets over Emerick and spun around to block sight of him, her hands on her hips.

Drest sprang onto the post and clambered up, up, to the beam embedded in the thatch. As long as no one looked there, she'd be safe. She pulled up her scabbard as the door creaked open.

"Ah! I beg your pardon." The knight slipped into the room and looked around with a greasy smile. "I saw this lad running, and I thought—oh, my, what a noddy I seem to be—but I thought he had something to tell me, and was trying to get me away from the rest."

Barbary let out a full-throated scream.

The knight flinched, and, still smiling, looked quickly around the hut again.

Drest held her breath. She would never forget that long forehead with its wreath of faint brown hair, that thin nose, those long flat cheeks, and those piercing dark eyes.

Nor the feel of his hand on her ankle, the sparkle of his blade in the night, and those horrible words in his cracked voice: *wolf's head.*

Tig advanced to the middle of the room. "If I'd something to tell you, I'd have stood outside and waited. You're not wanted here."

The knight stiffened. "Are those the words to speak to a guest of your village? I think not."

"I don't care what you think. Will you leave?"

The knight crossed his arms. "I may not care what *you* think, either, but I *do* care what you *know*. And I shall not leave until you tell me where *she* is. Now, will you do it here, or shall I take you outside?"

Tig didn't move.

Drest reached up into her tunic for her dagger.

Trust your friend. Nutkin's voice, a whisper. *He knows what to do.*

"Information," said Tig softly, "or a beating?"

"I think you'll find it best to do as I say."

"I don't like beatings, but perhaps it will be a beating that will go beyond bruises and cuts," Tig mused, as if he hadn't heard the knight. "I can't control it, though. The men will decide."

"What are you talking about?" snapped the knight. "What men?"

Tig's eyes met Wimarca's with a gaze suddenly keen and questioning.

The old healer rocked Barbary, and the bairn became quiet. "Do you know in what village you stand?" she said in a gentle voice, her gaze on the baby. "Its history of hatred against the men who come from Faintree Castle is long and bleak."

"*I* am no castle man, and *you*, old woman, had better—"

"They'll know you. They sniff it out, our villagers. And it won't be just men. No, every villager with a strong arm will have already gathered up their sticks, their hoes, their sickles, and will be coming to this hut. Yes, my dear." She smiled down at the baby. "They saw you leave. They saw where you hurried. And woe to you if they see you standing here."

Silence. The knight looked around the room, his eyes flicking over Elys and the table and the fire, returning to Wimarca, and then to Tig, who had raised his chin and was looking expectantly outside.

"You *will* answer me," snarled the knight, but he retreated, and soon was out the door.

Wimarca strode to the threshold and with her foot shoved the door closed. Mordag let out a long, harsh *creea*.

"He's waiting," Tig whispered. "He's just outside."

Barbary let out another wail, and this time, her mother went to her.

Mordag's call rang out again—but it wasn't from the roof now. It was farther away. Then it came again, still farther.

"He's run off, but not far." Tig rushed to the bed, where

Emerick had thrown back the blanket and was starting to rise. "Hurry! I'll help you."

Drest scampered down the post.

"Here, child." Wimarca thrust a cloak and hood into Drest's arms. "Put these on."

Tig was pulling Hodge's tunic over Emerick's torso as the young lord slipped his arms through the sleeves. Elys unbuckled her own belt and handed it wordlessly to Tig, who buckled it around Emerick's waist.

"I wonder if he noticed that you're wearing the castle's colors," Emerick said.

"Oh, I'm sure he did; he wouldn't have challenged me *quite* that much if he hadn't." Tig marched to the fire and lifted the pot. "One more drink, Emerick."

"There isn't time." Wimarca grabbed a bunch of herbs from her table and thrust them into Emerick's hand. "Chew these when you're in pain, but sparingly. Now all of you: Go. Before that man sees that no one's on the path and returns."

Drest darted to Emerick's side and slipped under his arm. Tig opened the door.

"It's safe," he whispered. "I think."

"Be careful, Tig—and you too, my lass," called Elys softly.

As Drest passed her, the woman reached out and

touched her cheek, a gentle stroke that Drest would remember later.

But at that moment, she hardly noticed. She was outside in the darkness, the shadows dense beneath the trees, and then she and Tig were running, Emerick heavy on her shoulder, into the woods.

-‹- 10 -›-

THE ESCAPE

"I doubt he's ever been to Brill's Gate; he must have seen it once on a map." Emerick shook his head. "No, he's not a tanner; his name is Sir Fergal. He's been at the castle for as long as I can remember. He was terrible on a horse and could not hit a target accurately with a sword *or* an arrow for his life. The master of the knights—Sir Reynard—gave him extra practice every day. Sir Fergal was always out in the bailey at midnight trying to get better at something or other."

They'd walked for hours, it seemed, until the partial moon was high, and had stopped to rest beside a mossy fallen trunk. The ground was damp.

"Sir Fergal," Drest said. The name was heavy in her mouth.

"I remember being in battle with him," Emerick went on. "I was kept in the back where there wasn't risk, and he was kept there too, as one of the knights we couldn't count on. I was fourteen years old, and he didn't speak to me once. I expect he was terrified as well."

"I'm sorry," said Drest. "I should have slain him when I had the chance."

"Then Wimarca and I wouldn't have had our bit of fun," said Tig with a hollow laugh. "Emerick, he didn't notice you, did he?"

Emerick reached into his tunic, where he had stuck the bundle of herbs, and withdrew a leaf. He'd been eating them slowly as he and his friends had fled, and the bundle was half gone. "I don't think so. With Elys's harsh look, I don't think he wanted to give our corner of the room much of a glance. And he didn't notice Drest. That's thanks to you, Tig. You made him hideously uncomfortable. Well done."

"I could have stopped him, though," said Drest.

"But you couldn't have stopped the whole village." Tig sighed. "You shouldn't have stayed in Phearsham Ridge." He raised his hands, then dropped them in his lap. "And now it's not safe for you anywhere. I'm sorry. I meant to keep my promise to protect you. Remember that from our last journey?"

Mordag was on Tig's shoulder and pressed hard against his cheek.

Drest leaned forward and wiped her palms on her hose. "I bet that Sir Fergal is going round to all the villages with

60

his tale of the price on my head. I should have called my brothers when I first saw him. I should have led him right to the mill, and they could have done him for me and I wouldn't need to worry about this."

"It does no good to talk like that." Emerick reached out with his boot and touched Drest's. "I said such words— what I *could* and *should* have done—every day for years after my sister died. It doesn't help. And as for Sir Fergal— he's a scoundrel, but it's good no one slew him when he first came to the village. If you hadn't made him chase you, you'd never have known about the price on your head. I know it's a hard burden to carry, but it's better to know than be ignorant."

Drest slept fitfully that night and woke at dawn with the ache in her forehead of a night spent tossing. She sat up and pressed her hands against her face, but the pressure did not cease.

Emerick was sprawled out by the log, his chest rising and falling with a catch. Tig was curled up by his legs, his breath more peaceful.

Drest crept away from them, leaving her cloak and hood behind. She was hot, desperately thirsty, and hungry.

A muddy brook gave her a mouthful of sour-tasting water that she spit out nearly at once. She wandered farther from her friends, searching the ground for traces of damp that might lead to a stream.

Then Drest caught a whiff of the sea.

The crisp, salty smell of home—

It was gone. The marshy reek of the woods surrounded her again.

Why don't you go home? Nutkin's voice. *You could stop running then.*

Drest's heart quickened. The headland was the one place where she knew how to hide. They could live there, the three of them, on the fish from the sea and the fresh water from the rain and be their own war-band. She would teach Emerick and Tig all that her brothers had taught her. They'd truly be safe.

Your lord is not going to want to live at the headland, Gobin scoffed. *Honestly, Drest, are you even going to mention that to him? He's a lord. He wants his castle back. The headland won't be enough.*

It'll have to be enough if he wants to heal in peace, Drest thought. *And he hasn't much of a choice if I'm going there.*

Emerick and Tig were sitting close together when she returned.

"—and that's its beauty. Its defenses are *impenetrable*."

Emerick looked up at Drest. "Nothing? We were hoping you'd find food."

"I was going to go after you," Tig faltered, "but I thought someone ought to stay with Emerick."

"Nay, I didn't find any food, but I have an idea." She knelt beside them. "Let's not wait here until any knights find us, but go to the headland. It's through the woods back there, and it has food and water and caves where we can hide."

Emerick and Tig exchanged glances.

"But my knights know how to get there," Emerick said. "Your caves won't be safe enough. And the castle will surely look for you there, knowing it was your camp and you'll likely go back for supplies."

"You've never seen the caves," Drest said coldly. "We can hide there no matter who comes."

Emerick looked at his hands. "Perhaps."

Tig nudged the young lord's elbow. "Tell her what you were telling me about the castle. Drest, it's magnificent. Just listen."

A smile crossed Emerick's face, making him look younger than his sixteen years. "You've seen it, Drest. Remember that long, open road that leads up to the first gatehouse? It allows room for no more than two horses abreast. And there are murder holes, and bowmen on all the battlements. It makes a trap."

"The paths on the headland are like traps for enemies," Drest muttered. "You don't know them the way I do."

"But a castle's traps—" Tig began, then stopped. "Did your father design all those defenses, Emerick? I remember how beautiful they were."

Strange word, sniffed Gobin's voice. *I didn't find any part of that castle beautiful.*

Emerick's smile faded. "My father liked to talk about his defenses, but he never called them beautiful. 'Useful.' 'Necessary.'" He was quiet for a moment. "No, he did call one 'beautiful.' That was my sister's marriage to Lord de Moys, which would have given us a link to the French throne. But my poor sister—Celestria died trying to escape that. If she'd married Lord de Moys, and if my own betrothal had gone through—I was to wed Lady Oriana Harkniss, whose family had ties to the Scottish throne—our father would have had the strongest alliance in the lowlands."

"Are you still betrothed?" asked Tig. "Have *you* ties with King William?"

"No. After Celestria died, Lord Harkniss had Oriana married to Lord de Moys and took that alliance for himself. I suppose Oriana thinks there's beauty in how it ended up: With Lord de Moys *and* Lord Harkniss dead and her with all that power. As for me, I haven't been betrothed to anyone for years."

"I don't think you will be anytime soon," Drest said. "No lady worth the name would want you without your castle."

It came out before she could stop it, from the resentment that had been building at Emerick's boasts of his secure castle and those alliances his family had almost had.

Emerick's mouth turned grim. "I expect you're right. I don't think anyone much wants me in this world."

"Aye, but it's better to be not wanted than to have everyone in the lowlands after your head." Drest stood. "The only place where I'll be safe is the headland. So will you come with me, or shall you stay on the run in the woods?"

"I don't see how the headland will be safe with all my knights—I mean, all *Oswyn's* knights—knowing precisely how to sail there in less than a day. No, Drest, I can't live like *that*."

"Bide your luck alone, then, and I'll bide mine." Drest shrugged at Tig, whose expression had become alarmed. "Perhaps I'll see you one day."

"You both—" Tig scrambled to his feet. "Honestly, if you two let yourselves part like that, neither one of you will forgive yourself!"

"Part like what? We're looking at the truth of the matter. I can't hope for any helpful alliance, being without a castle as I am; and she's got to run for her life, being a wolf's—"

"Stop it!" Tig whirled to Emerick. "Don't ever say those words again."

Emerick reddened.

She almost marched away. That was her instinct.

But another instinct held her there—and a memory of a journey not long ago.

And it was that which made her walk to Emerick's side and drop on her knees and wait until he looked at her before she spoke.

"I have to find somewhere to live," she said. "I can't be like my da, always running. There's no other place for me but the headland."

"And it's your home," he said softly.

"If I go and find it's safe, will you come? I want you to come."

He hesitated, then slowly nodded. And then he reached over and put his arm around her.

"Be careful, Drest. And be sure you come back."

She hugged him, and stood.

"Shall I go with you?" asked Tig. "I've never seen the headland."

"Nay, stay with Emerick. He might need you and Mordag. I'll be back as soon as I can."

And forcing a faded smile at her friends, Drest started into the woods alone.

⤛ 11 ⤜

THE HEADLAND

*H*ome, said a voice deep in Drest's mind. *You're going home.*

She hadn't been back to the headland since she had left with Emerick after the knights' invasion a week ago. But she knew the way. It was simple: straight through the woods to the shore, then along the water.

Her limbs longed to sprint, but Drest forced herself to stride to keep her pace steady and not tire.

Your home has better defenses than the castle of that squid-brained pig's bottom. It was Uwen's voice.

Aye, said Gobin. *The dragons' teeth all over the coves. What does Da always say? They're always hungry for wood and men.*

The cliffs that no man can climb, said Nutkin. *No man but us.*

The ravine and its river. The rough sea. It's as fine as a castle's defense. Gobin laughed. *She really* could *keep her poor lord safe there for the rest of his life.*

She could.

Drest's pace increased into a full run as she pictured it:

The path to the lookout point, Emerick and Tig at her side, the sea stretching vast and gray around them.

The bonfire at the camp, fish roasting on the coals, firelight flickering on Emerick's face as he told stories of his youth in his castle voice.

They'd sleep in the caves where it was safe.

She'd teach them to dive off the cliffs, and how to swim.

They'd battle with practice swords on the paths.

And Mordag would keep watch upon the wind.

The vast sea.

The broad stones.

Her home.

Her life.

Drest had been in the woods for an hour when the first full breath of the sea wafted through the trees. Water glimmered in the distance, slats of light against the dark trunks. Drest dashed up to the brink of the woods, taking in the rich, briny smell and the sharp feel of the sea air. Waves slapped at the pebble shore below her.

She breathed deep.

Then she returned to the trees. Had she come this way with Emerick? Until a week ago, she'd never been off the headland. She recognized nothing, but her mind flew back to those days in the woods by the headland—when everything had been unfamiliar, and she and Emerick had

69

exchanged hostilities. His sneer, his wince, and his hopeless gaze rose in her mind.

I need you, he'd said. *And you need me. And that's all we must remember.*

She continued, following the shore, heading north. Her boots crunched the white shells tossed up by storms. Sea wind cooled her hot, sticky back.

Another hour passed. Her energy waned. She found a stream and drank deeply.

Another hour.

She was starting to wonder if the woods would ever turn familiar when, abruptly, the land before her was gone, replaced by a thundering cove.

Drest marched up to the edge of the cliff and leaned over. Waves crashed below, flicking up foam, speckling her tunic with damp.

This was the start of the ravine, the slash in the headland where she had found Emerick just over a week ago. Beyond it, over the waves, sat the slabs of boulders that were the entry to the headland itself.

The cliff at her feet was ragged—perfect for climbing— and Drest dropped to her knees, about to start down.

But she paused.

The sea below was rich with foam, pitted with dragons'

teeth, and rabid with waves. Such waves on such stones did not bode well for climbing.

Nutkin had once said that there was a way down. But he'd never told her where, or how.

She followed the ravine deeper into the woods, along the cliffs.

A way that Nutkin would make, Gobin's voice whispered, *would look like no way at all.*

She examined the ground. Roots, acorns, leaves, and fallen branches scattered the soil, but with no answer to Gobin's riddle.

And then she passed an enormous root extending from an oak, reaching under the leaves and over the cliff's edge, a pale, twining root that she wouldn't have noticed, only the tip of her boot brushed it—and instead of being solid wood, it was soft.

Drest followed it up to the oak and discovered that it was looped and tied around the trunk.

Not a root but a rope.

Drest grinned. The knot was Gobin's work and the arrangement of leaves at the base of the oak Nutkin's. And the groove in the dirt, where the rope rested root-like as it snaked down to the cliff, was the work they'd done together.

Drest knelt and lifted the rope from the dirt, then peered

over the brink of the cliff. The rope extended all the way to the bottom. Slowly, taking care, she eased herself over the cliff's edge.

Her feet found solid holds in the first swath of rock. She descended quickly.

Why does Da call this the cliff no man can climb? Uwen's voice. *It's an easy climb down, at least for a bug-headed spider like you.*

Bits of rocks flew away from her boots as she shuttled down, then chunks of moss. Now heavy layers of moss covered the cliff face, holding her feet nearly as well as pitted stone.

And then—

Drest's boot slipped.

Her toes scrabbled. For the first time in her life, she found no hold.

The rope was all that was supporting her. Drest clung to it and looked down.

A cliff of slick, glistening stone stretched below, a rock face smoothed by hundreds of years of rain dripping from the moss.

Tentatively, Drest slid her toe down the rock. There were no crannies, no cracks or ledges, nothing in which to gain a hold. She had but one choice: to climb down that rope alone.

It was hard to descend like that, inching along, but Drest made herself do it. Hand over hand, foot over foot, minute after minute, the rough fibers digging into her palms. Rope was not like cliff; it was restrictive to her muscles. She felt like a slithering drop of water.

When the rope ended, four feet above the ground, Drest let go and landed in a crouch on the ravine's floor.

All around her, a faint mist rose. It was quiet and dark.

But familiar.

It was the world she had grown up in.

With tears in her eyes, she strode toward the seaside bank and climbed up into the foggy sun at the top.

Great stone slabs stretched everywhere, forming a rocky landscape of gullies and hills, the sea a brimming mass of gray-green beyond. To all eyes, it was but a rock for seabirds and seals, nothing else. It was the core of the headland's defense.

A brilliant defense! Gobin's voice rang out in her mind. *No one will see you here. It's perfect, lass, just perfect!*

And yet—now that she was there, it looked different somehow.

That wide-open sea beyond the stones was not a barrier, but a path on which enemy ships could travel.

The cliff that no one could climb would keep her in as well if the rope were gone.

The paths were bare, without protection, and anyone standing on them would be obvious from the sea.

As she stood on the edge of the stone path, the wind whipping against her face and tunic, Drest remembered how the wind had felt on the road leading up to Faintree Castle.

A wind above cliffs and a road with a massive stone fortress at its end.

The headland feels—wrong.

Has your mind turned into a rotten turnip? Uwen's voice. *How can it feel wrong?*

Because this is where it began. Wulfric's solemn voice. *It's where Da and the rest of us were captured. It's not safe for you here, lass. Go back.*

Drest shook her head. It *had* been safe until that day. Surely it was safe now.

She began marching up toward the lookout point.

The wind turned cold.

Nay, lass, it's not safe. Thorkill, nervous, as he'd rarely been. *Go and fetch some smoked fish, but then go back to your friends. Do it quick and leave.*

With a shiver, Drest pivoted—

But not before she caught the glimpse of a movement past the curve on the path toward the lookout point.

And in seconds, he was before her: a craggy old knight

in a tree-emblazoned surcoat that flapped in the wind, staring down at her with pale blue eyes like Emerick's.

She'd seen that face once before, at the top of the battlements of Faintree Castle's inner curtain wall. She would have known that face anywhere.

Sir Oswyn.

←← 12 →→

THE CLIFF

Drest stumbled back, back, nearly tripping on a loose clump of gorse.

"Crossbows!" bellowed Sir Oswyn.

She bolted down the nearest bank into the ravine. With a shower of pebbles and dirt in her wake, Drest reached the bottom and sprinted toward the cliff.

Someone shouted in the distance. Soil and stones crashed as castle men rushed into the ravine after her.

Drest wove between trees, focusing only on her speed and her direction, trying to remember where on the cliff the rope was waiting.

This was the most important race of her life. She all but flew.

At last, the cliff rose ahead, and the rope—there it was, dangling pale against the stone not far away.

Drest ran at the cliff and jumped, praying she would reach the rope's fraying end.

Her fingers closed around the tip.

With a grunt, her boots slipping against the slick rock, her arms straining, she pulled herself up, hand over hand, until her boots caught the rope at the end.

"Halt!" cried a thin, cold voice from below, coming near: Sir Oswyn's.

How had he caught up so quickly?

That old man is fast, mused Gobin.

Climb, lass, climb! Nutkin's voice.

She gritted her teeth and pulled herself higher, Tancored in its scabbard thumping against her leg, her boots steadying her, though her arms alone carried her weight.

"Should I shoot, sir?" came a younger voice.

"Stay ready, Ewart. You there! Halt, and tell me where you've put my nephew's body!"

He's pretending for the bowman that you killed the lord, murmured Gobin's voice. *But he's also asking you where you're hiding him.*

"Halt at once! We've a crossbow trained on your back and you've a price on your head!"

Drest quailed, but did not stop climbing. If that bowman let loose a bolt—

"God's *blood,*" said the younger voice. "Look at her go."

"Now!" Sir Oswyn.

There was a familiar muted *thump*—a crossbow firing.

Drest flung her body to the left, still clinging to the rope.

A bolt slammed against the rock face inches from her hand. It hovered there, then fell.

Had she not swung away, that iron tip would have plunged between her shoulders.

"Are you listening?" roared Sir Oswyn. "Climb down and I will spare your life!"

"God's bones, she's going to fall!" said the younger voice.

God's bones, Drest, keep climbing!

Emerick's voice.

Drest lunged for a new hold. She hauled herself up, hand over hand. Her mind was numb, but her instinct was alive again and forcing her on.

"Load your weapon!"

A scrape, a fumble.

"Faster, Ewart! If this beast will not tell us where she's hidden my nephew, she shall die. Halt, villain! Do you hear me? Halt, or my man will shoot, and he'll not miss this time!"

There was too much cliff. The bowman *would* shoot again before she reached the top.

Thorkill's voice came into her mind, tense, as if he were beside her:

You have five seconds, lass. It takes me five seconds to load a crossbow. Do you remember? Five seconds to put my foot in the stirrup and pull back the string.

Hand over hand, a relentless rhythm.

He's putting the string on its hold. Thorkill. *He's setting in the bolt.*

Drest, try a drop-and-grab. Nutkin's voice, pleading. *Remember how I taught you that when we were climbing ropes?*

"Now!"

Another muted *thump*.

Drest released the rope, ducking as she did so, and grabbed the rough fibers again, a foot below where she had held them before.

Nicely done! Nutkin called.

The bolt slammed into the cliff directly beside the rope, spraying bits of stone.

"My *God*," said the lighter voice. "How did she do *that*?"

Five seconds to load. Thorkill's voice. *Hurry, lass.*

She hauled herself up, passing her former hold.

Hand over hand, as fast as she had ever climbed.

And then she was at the swath of moss. The rough part that led to the top was above it.

Drest dug her feet into the moss, and propelled herself up, even faster now.

The rock changed. It was weathered stone at last, pitted with cracks and ledges.

"Now!" cried Sir Oswyn.

The muted *thump*.

Her boot caught a ledge at once, and her fingers found

grips. Drest sprang to the side, off the rope entirely, and clung to the rough rock face.

The bolt crashed against the stone beside her—into the rope itself, cutting it. Both bolt and rope fell, one after the other.

Drest reached for the crack above her head.

Five seconds.

Drest, you climb like a spider. Nutkin's voice.

Four seconds.

Come on, you rabbit-headed—climb! Uwen's voice.

Three seconds.

Never falter before yourself or the enemy. Wulfric's voice.

Two.

Drest, come back to me. Emerick's voice.

One.

She was at the top, her fingers pressing into the dirt and dead leaves mounded on the rocky edge. She hauled herself up and rolled toward the trees.

Thump.

The bolt thudded against the cliff at the brink, spraying dirt—and fell back.

Drest sprang to her feet and did not give the bowman a chance for another shot. She plunged into the woods.

⤙ 13 ⤚

THE USE OF A CASTLE

Drest ran wildly, without direction at first, swamped with the relief of her escape—but also with the despair of her failure. No place would be safe for her again. She would always have to run.

And yet—she was tired. Desperately so.

She slowed her pace and continued toward Phearsham Ridge at a walk.

Wolf's head, hummed her steps. *Nearly caught, wolf's head.*

Her brothers' voices were silent.

Drest plodded on, pausing only to kneel at a brook and take deep gulps of the cold, clean water, and to soak her hands to numb the rawness.

There was still light when the fallen log came into view. Tig and Emerick sat with their legs stretched out beside one another, as if they'd done nothing but talk all that day. Yet as she neared, she saw how weary their faces were, and pale. Though both faces brightened at the sight of her.

"It's not safe on the headland, just as Emerick thought,"

Drest said, her voice breaking. "I'll tell you more, but let me fetch us something to eat first."

"Wait." Tig sprang up and strode to her side. "Mordag and I can do that. I'm just as good in the woods as you, remember? And you look as if you could use a rest."

Drest ran her hand through her hair. The ragged clumps were damp with sweat to their tips. "What are you going to hunt with? If I lend you my dagger, do you promise not to lose it?"

"I don't need your dagger. If you stay here with Emerick, I'll creep back to Phearsham Ridge and fetch us a *proper* sack of food."

Drest shook her head. "Nay, it's not safe. Nothing's safe. What if you went, lad, and that knight was still there?"

"I can creep in the woods unseen. I'm as good at *that* as your brothers, you know. And you—you need to sit and close your eyes. You walked there and back, didn't you, without a break." He reached forward as if to grasp her shoulder, but his fingers only grazed it. "Let me help. Please?"

She drew him into a rough hug, like the kind Uwen had given her. "Be careful," she whispered into the tickle of his black hair.

"I will." His breath warmed her neck before he pulled away. "Now go and rest. I command it."

She staggered to the log and collapsed in Tig's place

beside Emerick. "Bring back some of that hearth bread your sister makes, will you? And cheese."

"And ale and a roast of some kind," Emerick said.

Tig bowed to them. "I'll be back before dark with more than you can eat."

With a click of his tongue, he set off into the woods, Mordag swooping above him.

Drest and Emerick sat in silence together. After Tig had disappeared completely behind the trees, she closed her eyes.

"Was it bad at the headland?"

"Aye."

"Were you seen by—by our enemies?"

"Aye."

"But you escaped." Emerick lifted one of her hands and laced his fingers with hers. "If I'm not mistaken, the stickiness on your hand is blood."

"Aye. It always bleeds when I climb rope."

"There's a rope on the headland?"

"On the cliff no man can climb."

He was quiet. "A cliff that *you* climbed, though."

"Aye."

He lifted her hand to his heart, and held it there. "I'm sorry, Drest."

A wild despair rose in her, increasing like a spring pond, until a bubble of a sob came to her lips.

"I saw your uncle," she managed to get out.

"My *God*," Emerick whispered.

"He asked where you were. He pretended you were dead for his man, but I knew what he meant. And he had his man shoot a crossbow at me."

"Oh, Drest, I can't even imagine—this is no life, this is— if you had died—" He reached around her and held her tight, pressing his face against her hair.

Somehow, it helped, that crushing, tremulous embrace. For the first time since she had heard Sir Fergal's horrible words, Drest felt truly safe.

And when Emerick loosened his grip, she told him everything. He never let her hand go even once as she spoke.

"I don't know what we can do now," Drest finished, a lump in her throat. "Da's on the run, Phearsham Ridge isn't safe, and your uncle—I don't know what he'll do next, but he's not giving up. He's going to hunt us both until we're dead."

"May I tell you something?" Emerick asked. "All while you were gone, Tig and I were plotting how to keep you safe. And here's what we came up with: You need a castle."

"You haven't got a castle."

"No, *I* haven't. But—" He hesitated. "Oriana Harkniss— Lady de Moys—*does*. She also has an army."

Silence.

"But you're not—what's that word?"

"Betrothed? No, I'm not, but she was Celestria's greatest friend when they were young. And after her husband died, she was my father's ally. I haven't thought about her for years. It was Tig who asked if she was *my* ally, and of course she is, and he—he wondered if she might help me."

Drest sat up. "Regain your castle, you mean?"

"Yes. She's the only way I could regain my castle, I fear. And if I'm lord again, I can end your sentence and stop this curse upon you."

"Will she help you?" Drest thought for a moment. "Will her army slay your uncle?"

Emerick bit his lip. "She might order her men to. And she has two armies. One's at her husband's castle—that's Mont-de-Roche, across the sea—and the other's at her father's castle, Harkniss, where she is now. She's master of both castles, and both armies. Her holdings are at least twice the size of my own." His face grew thoughtful. "I'd never have asked her help in a million years, but I'll do it for you."

"Why do you say that? Do you not like her?"

"No, it's not that, it's just—Drest, she's hardly my friend. If I beg her in Celestria's name, she *might* help. But I'll have to be on my knees, my face in the dirt, admitting that I am a worm compared to—no, let's not think of that. Let's think only of reaching her—for when we do, if she agrees, we'll have the most powerful person in the lowlands at our side."

A tiny hope grew inside Drest, like a breath of air. "Is Harkniss Castle in the lowlands?"

"Yes, it's north of here, not far. Two days' walk, I expect."

"Are its defenses as impressive as your own?"

Emerick bit back a smirk. "Not quite, but they're good enough. And there's a secret passageway inside the walls, leading all over and to the postern gate. Oriana once locked me in there when we were children."

Drest was on her knees. "Can you walk for two days?"

"I should hope so. I've had a full day of rest here with Tig. I may open all my wounds again, but surely Oriana has a healer. And as that witch from Soggyweald told me, I'm young and have a strong frame and *ought* to be able to live. Remember that?"

Drest grinned. "Aye. Merewen. I was angry with her for not healing you."

"Yes, you were glowering all that way back to the road. I remember thinking, *God's bones, she doesn't hate me as much as I thought she did.*"

"Nay, I never hated you. I was only doing what I had to do."

Emerick's smile faded. "And being who you had to be. As was I. God's breath, we've really been through a lot together, haven't we."

And they settled back, shoulder by shoulder, to wait for Tig.

And waited.

And waited still more.

Before it was dark, Drest and Emerick staggered off to find a stream. It was an hour before they did, but then they each drank deeply. On their way back to the log, Drest found a patch of sour brambleberries and picked the lot of them.

Tig was not waiting at the fallen moss-covered tree.

Emerick settled down and took a stem from the herbs in his tunic. "Drest, we should start for Harkniss. I don't think Tig is coming back." He hesitated. "He's met trouble. And Oswyn saw you. We have no time to lose."

Drest curled up against the log, pulling her knees into her arms. "I should have gone with Tig. He's done something foolish, trying to be brave."

"Or he's doing something brave right now," said Emerick. "If Sir Fergal is still there, Tig might be staying so that he doesn't lead him straight to you."

⊷ 14 ⊷

THE ONLY WAY

Drest and Emerick headed north through the woods. For hours they trudged onward. The air grew cold. Emerick began leaning on Drest, and she draped her cloak over both of them to keep them warm. When the moon was high, they slept beside a cliff strewn with ragged trees.

At dawn, Drest left Emerick and went off to hunt and came back with a hare.

"The last time we traveled together, your bandit ate our hare," Emerick said as they watched the skinned carcass cook on its stick of a spit over the fire that Drest had built.

She edged closer to her friend. "I hope he's not in these woods. If he knows the price on my head—"

"I doubt he'd take it." But Emerick shifted closer to her until their shoulders touched. "Being in these woods at dawn makes me think of two things: you and our journey to my castle, and going on a hunt when I was younger. I don't know if my mind is conjuring this, but I could swear I know these woods."

"You and I didn't travel here before; it's too far north."

"Yes, I know. So if I truly remember it, it's woods I've seen before."

A dollop of fat dripped from the hare and sizzled in the fire.

"If I'm right," Emerick went on, "the cliff behind us isn't very deep, with a stream at the bottom. Then past those trees, there's a bog."

"Shall I see about the cliff?"

He nodded, and Drest rose and peered over the cliff's edge.

Water glimmered below.

"Emerick, there's a wee beck down there! Can you climb a cliff? I'll help you down—"

"Not in this state; I'd never be able to make it up again. Drest, you go. You must drink."

She hesitated for only a few seconds, then scampered over the edge of the cliff and down.

It was a crumbling face of rock. She remembered all that Nutkin had taught her about climbing with unsteady holds. And though her palms were still raw from the rope at the headland, her fingertips—what she needed for cliffs—barely stung.

The stream was deeper than it had seemed from the top of the cliff, and the water was smooth, clean, and icy against her teeth and palms.

The last time I traveled, I drank from old tree trunks and muddy puddles.

Aye, but you found them when you needed them and you met your thirst, said Thorkill. *Your poor friend, though. He'll not do well on the walk tomorrow if he doesn't drink.*

Drest sat up and wiped the water from her face. *What shall I do? I cannot hold water in my hands as I climb.*

You could dip your cloak in this beck and squeeze it out in his mouth.

She lifted the corner of the cloak. It was spattered with mud. *Nay, I can't do that to him.*

Perhaps you could find something in the beck. Something that could carry water.

Drest walked a few steps farther down the stream and stuck her hand into a place where the pebbles had mounded by the force of the water. One by one, she took out the largest stones, but none had an indentation deep enough to carry water. She was about to give up and dip the least muddy part of her cloak into the stream when her fingers grazed a thin stone that curved.

A thin stone that extended out, and rounded.

Carefully, Drest removed all the pebbles around that one, and soon the stream had washed away enough mud to reveal her find:

A clay jug.

It was broken at the lip and filled with silt and pebbles, but the base showed no cracks. Drest filled it, wedged it into her sword-belt, then slowly climbed back up the cliff.

For a moment, she didn't see Emerick, or the fire. A swift, sour fear seized her: that the bandit Jupp had returned and had stolen their hare again, and this time slain her friend.

But then she saw him, lying on the ground, his figure blocking the glow from the flames.

"I've water for you," Drest said.

Emerick sat up. "How?"

"I found a jug. Someone who was hunting here must have gone down to fill it and forgotten it." She drew it from her belt and pressed it into his hands.

"It's amazing how a simple jug can make life seem so much brighter," Emerick said when he was finished drinking. "Is it too much to ask for you to fill this again?"

"Nay, and I shall fill it before we leave so we'll have something to drink as we walk."

"God's bones, that's a vast improvement over our past journeys together. One day, Drest, we shall have to plan like your father and pack supplies."

Da. "I wonder where he is."

"Running. Hiding. I'm sorry, Drest; I shouldn't have

asked for you to stay in the village. You should be with your family."

If you'd come with us, lass, we'd be protecting you, said Wulfric.

Aye, but then I'd be always running.

And what are you doing now? sneered Uwen's voice. *Sitting by a fire in a nice cozy hut telling stories? You're not a wolf's head but a boar's head for putting yourself on the run like this, wearing yourself out taking care of your soggy lord—*

I'm not running, you hairy fish's bladder! I'm on my way to a castle to get an army to get back Emerick's castle. Aye, and when I see you next, it'll be from the battlements—and I'll make you kneel to me, you pockmarked, lumpy slug!

And yet as Drest climbed down the cliff to fill the jug again, she was so tired she almost slipped.

When they'd finished the hare, they set off. Their pace was even swifter, for Emerick really *did* know the way, remembering a magnificent tall elm, an old Scots pine that had been uprooted in a storm, and then the bog.

The ground was damp and sticky, but soon they were past and into sparse woods. In places, bare tree roots had risen bone-like through washed-away soil.

After several hours, they rested and took turns sipping from the jug.

"How close are we to Harkniss?" Drest asked.

"If you can believe it, we may be there by midday tomorrow."

They went on until it was dark, and Emerick slept. But not Drest.

If Tig was hurt, I'd know, wouldn't I? I'd feel it somehow.

None of her brothers' voices answered.

Drest frowned and turned over, wincing as her scabbard poked into her.

Tig wouldn't be hurt. He was clever and swift, and he was right: He could hide in the woods as well as any of her brothers.

And yet as she lay there, she could see Tig by the mill, packing bread and cheese and meat into a sack, and Sir Fergal approaching silently behind him.

Nay, Mordag would warn him. And Elys would be there. Aye, Elys would help.

Elys, whose embrace had felt like a mother's might: all-surrounding and safe. Just as her hand had felt on Drest's cheek before they'd parted.

Was that what a mother was like? Her real mother wasn't even a shadowy memory. Grimbol had never told Drest who her mother had been, nor her brothers, and Drest had never thought to ask. It was as if her mother never *had* been.

I wonder if she'd like me as much as Elys seems to.

"Are you nervous as well?" Emerick. A faint whisper.

Drest crawled silently to his side. "Do you mean about the castle?"

"Yes. Drest, I—I haven't seen Oriana in years. Since before she was married." His voice grew softer. "She never liked me. I was only Celestria's little brother. I was always too small and too—too weak for her to respect."

"Emerick, you're grown now."

"But I've lost my castle and my army and *everything* within months of inheriting them. How could she respect me? When her husband died, she took over *two* castles and *two* armies without blinking an eye." He shuddered. "What if she sneers at me and says that a man so weak should never have a castle? What if she takes my castle for her own and turns me out?"

"Nay, she won't, not if she's your ally."

His face was troubled. "I didn't tell you the truth before. I *have* thought of Lady de Moys. Just not recently. Before I went to the headland to capture your family, some of my knights told me I should ask for her help. I said no. Why would I need *her* help? Did *I* not have a strong army of my own? I don't want to ask for her help now. I should be able to do this on my own, only—only I can't."

Gently, Drest took his hand.

He was shaking. "Will you stay with me when I speak with her? It will be good for Oriana to see you and to know that I'm not completely friendless in this world. Or completely pitiful."

"You're not pitiful. You've had bad luck; that's all." Drest leaned against him. "And you're not friendless. Even if you were once, you'll never be that again."

⤙ 15 ⤚

THE GATEHOUSE

A watery sun woke Drest, and with it came a sense of dread. Today they would arrive at Harkniss Castle. Today Lady de Moys would agree to help them—or reject their pleas. Or worse: She might take advantage of Emerick's weakness. And then the wolf's head would be with Drest forever.

They staggered on through the brightness of morning. Emerick kept up with Drest's pace, though he was panting. It was past midday when he asked to stop at a golden wheat field that seemed to glow beyond the trees.

But when they came to the field, they saw where it ended: in the near distance at a long, towering wall. Within the wall rose a brutal gray block of a fortress.

"Oh," said Emerick, sounding as if his word had crept from deep in the ground. "We're here. Harkniss Castle."

Two spear-bearing guards in helms and brown tunics stopped them at the gate.

"Your business?" said one, his eyes flicking between them.

Drest had donned the cloak and hood to hide her sword

and most of her face. The guard's gaze slid off her and fixed on Emerick, who was sweating and pale.

"We—we've come for an audience with Lady de Moys," he stammered. "Is she—is she seeing anyone today?"

"Yesterday was Petition Day," the guard said. "You're too late."

Emerick's posture wilted. "May I send her a word?"

"Nay, you can't do that. But you can wait for Petition Day next week."

The other guard nudged the first with flat of his spear. "He could send word, couldn't he? Just to ask?"

"Has the lady ever seen a villager outside of Petition Day? Nay, she hasn't. Were I him, I wouldn't waste my time."

"But I'm not one of her villagers," Emerick blurted. "I'm her friend, an old friend from many years ago."

Now both guards were frowning.

"What's your name?" said the first.

"E—Edric. Edric of Weemsdale."

"Weemsdale isn't one of the lady's villages," said the first guard slowly. "Strange. I don't think she's ever been there."

Above their heads, a hawk that had been circling the bailey let out a piercing shriek.

Emerick flinched.

Now the guards were staring. The first had lowered his

spear. The second had set his foot to the side, in what Drest knew well was a balancing position, ready to fight.

She suppressed an urge to throw back her cloak and draw her sword.

"Everyone the lady's kind to thinks she's their friend," Drest said. She cleared her throat. "She was kind to Edric long ago, when he was but a lad. She was kind to my da too. He fought for Lord de Moys as a man-at-arms. He told me I should see her if I was ever in need. And I am."

The guards glanced at each other.

The sun beat down on her hood and cloak.

"That's different," said the first guard. "If your da fought for the lord's army, she'll listen to you."

The second guard pointed into the bailey with his spear. "Go ahead. Find someone to take your message to her. Make sure you say your da's name, the name of a battle he fought with Lord de Moys, and what your need is. She doesn't see petitioners outside of her one day, but she'll do it for a lass with that connection."

"But go to the well first," said the first guard. "Your Edric there seems parched."

"Thank you." Drest took Emerick's hand and led him away from the gatehouse and onto the grass of the bailey.

"Oh, God," breathed Emerick, "I didn't know what to say. I can't do this."

"Nay, you can. We're in, are we not? Do you see the well?"

Everything in the bailey distracted her. This green was different from Faintree Castle's expanse of grass: This was a town between the walls.

A tannery belched foul odors nearby into a river by the guardhouse. Smoke floated up from a smithy. Loud clanging sounded from there too. Across the path, rich scents of bread and meat wafted from a cookhouse.

And the people—as many as had been in Launceford, clustering, gossiping, rushing, forming a sea of faces.

And then Drest's breath stopped in her throat.

Not more than four sword lengths away stood a knight in a white surcoat with a bold blue tree: the colors of Faintree Castle.

Emerick ducked close. "That's Sir Roland, one of Oswyn's most trusted men. I don't know what this means. If he recognizes me—"

"Let's hide."

"No, I—you go on. I'll hide at the tannery. There's some shade there, and no one will question me if I'm resting. Find Lady de Moys and tell her where I am, or—or beg her yourself for what we need and—just go!" Emerick staggered back toward the buildings clustered near the end of the curtain wall.

He'd left her. There, alone in the bailey, with a knight who surely knew of the wolf's head curse.

You're not my friend but a filthy coward, Drest thought.

The Faintree Castle knight was still standing on the path, idly, as if he were simply out enjoying the sun. His eyes were drifting around the yard. They flicked on Drest, then away—but then came back.

"You there. Do I know you?"

"No, sir," said Drest slowly.

"You were staring at me."

"I—didn't mean to, sir."

Her chest was tight. There was no room to draw her sword, nor room to run.

A hand closed over her arm.

"There you are, dawdling as you do," said a woman's stern voice. "Come along, before I lose my temper."

And a hard grip pulled her back into the crowd.

The knight grinned and looked away.

Drest looked up at her rescuer.

And nearly let out a cry.

In a humble shift and apron with a modest cap holding back all her hair was the vengeful woman she had saved from an angry mob and fiery death at Soggyweald:

The witch and healer Merewen.

→ 16 →

THE HEALER

Merewen swept through the crowd, her hand clamped on Drest's wrist, leading her to a small hut set back on the grass between a cluster of others like it. Drest ducked through the low doorway after her and blinked in the dim light.

It was a tiny room, its floor strewn with trodden brown rushes, with a ring of stones for a fire in the center. Rolled-up blankets, a line of jugs, and a woven basket teeming with sausages hung from the walls.

Merewen pushed Drest deeper in and stood by the door.

Drest clasped her hands. "Is he gone?"

"Yes." Merewen turned back and sighed. "You, child, take too many risks."

She drew the door shut and stepped over to a tall chest piled high with herb bundles. She gestured for Drest to sit on the mounded rushes at its base. The witch sank to her side and stared at her in silence.

Drest stared back. She had saved the witch's life, but Merewen had saved Drest's life at Faintree Castle with the

101

cloak that had hidden Emerick and helped her and her friends to escape.

"Thank you for your help on the road," Drest said at last.

Amusement flickered in Merewen's face. "Did my cloak aid you on your journey? I expect it did; the sky seemed to break open with rain that night."

"Aye, and it helped me and Tig get away from the castle. With Emerick." Drest paused. "He's the injured knight I was traveling with. He's really Lord Faintree. I learned that later."

Merewen's eyes narrowed. "He tricked you into taking him all that way? I hear he's dead now."

"Nay, he's not dead. And he's my friend. He's hiding by the tannery. He needs to see the lady of this castle." Drest wavered. "Nay, *I* need to see the lady of this castle. *He's* hiding."

Merewen's gaze softened. "Not dead, and your friend. Well. Is he still wounded? I would think so, given how he looked when I saw him last. I might be able to help this time." She reached up to the chest and took down a bundle of herbs. She untied them and began to sort the stems on her lap.

"Are you the healer here?"

"I am one of several healers here. This hut belongs to a sister in my trade, but I'll not stay here long; it is neither safe for me nor my stag. My poor stag; he's wandering those woods alone."

Drest remembered the stag: a majestic beast with a crown of antlers like a king.

"But to meet *you* here—" Merewen gave a faint smile. "I've thought of nothing *but* you since I left you with that cloak on the road to Faintree Castle. And here you are. How strange chance is."

Merewen reached out and set her cold, long-fingered hand against Drest's cheek and held it there.

It was not like Elys's hand: gentle, rough, but kind. This was a hand that had clenched in anger, had torn and thrust, a hand that had set all the thatch in her village aflame.

Drest flinched, and the hand dropped away. "I need to see the lady of the castle."

"So you said. Why?"

"We need her army. Emerick's uncle is holding his castle against him and—"

"Where is Grimbol? This should be *his* task."

"Nay, Da only wants to keep afoot and hide. But I can't." Drest took a deep breath. "There's a price on my head."

"Like on your father's."

"Nay, I'm—I'm a wolf's head."

Merewen's eyes widened, then narrowed at once. "Who made that so?" Her voice was a low rumble, like thunder.

Drest's face reddened. "Emerick's uncle. But it doesn't matter. I need to find the lady, because then we'll have her army, and then—then Emerick can get back his castle and take away that sentence."

"A sentence like that is not easy to end. Child, do you know what this means? If you are called a wolf's head, every town in the lowlands will hear. And every lad, lass, woman, and man will hunger for the coins they'd get if they were to cause your death."

Drest swallowed. "I know. That's why I need to go to Emerick's castle. I can hide, and—"

"Will you hide there all your life? Ah, child. They know of you even here: the bloodthirsty lass who freed the Mad Wolf from Faintree Castle's prison. And they say that Lord Faintree died by *your* hand."

Drest picked up a rush from the floor and rubbed it between her fingers. "Tig always said I was a legend."

"Tig was right. But you bear a new legend now, and it will doom you if you are not careful. A castle will not protect you from it, unless you stay behind the castle's walls forever. A castle will swiftly change from your sanctuary to your prison. And every person within will never forget what you are."

"I've no choice, do I? It's that or always running like my da—"

"There *is* another way." Merewen set down her stems, her hand shaking. "Transform yourself. Become not the Mad Wolf's daughter but a simple village lass. Bury your sword in the woods. I'll find you a cap to hide your hair and a shift. Stay with me. Be my apprentice, and no one will question us. Yes, child, that's how I'll save your life this time."

Drest stared at the witch's intense silver eyes.

She could be like Idony, a lass with a quiet life in a village.

No running. No fear. Just a simple life in a hut.

Her brothers could visit as they fled from place to place.

And Emerick—he could go with her and become a village lad. He'd never gain his castle back, but he could live without fear as well.

And so could Tig.

But going into that life would mean giving up everything you've ever been, murmured Gobin. *Could you really leave it all?*

Her sword.

Her old legend.

Be yourself, Drest, Wulfric had said when they had last parted. As if he'd known of the choice that would be before her.

Honestly, lass, do you think life with a woman who burns villages in revenge would be all that peaceful? Nutkin's voice.

But it might save your life. Thorkill. *Don't say nay too quickly.*

And then Drest thought of Emerick hiding by the tannery, pale with fear, transformed into a coward by the sight of his own man.

And of Tig, who was still missing.

They needed her to be herself.

She needed to be herself.

Drest's hand drifted down to Tancored and brushed the pommel. "Nay, I can't give up my sword. Do you know the lady of this castle?"

Merewen drew back. "No. I saw her for the first time this morning. She was giving her troops orders, sending them off."

"Sending them off?" Drest echoed. "To where?" It was almost too much to hope that she could be sending them to Faintree Castle, and yet—

"To defend against a foe in the western lands."

The hope began to dwindle. "Emerick said she had more men in her army than his uncle, so—so maybe she hasn't sent *all* her knights away."

"I do not know." Merewen took a deep breath. "Must you go into that castle? Bring your friend here. I will take you both away, to somewhere remote, where no one can find you. My stag and I—we will do all in our power to protect you." She paused. "I cannot let you go again."

Merewen's final words were soft, but a sharp warning slid down Drest's spine.

She bolted to her feet. "I need to get into that castle. Thank you for your help, but I don't want any more of it."

"It's not safe for you out there—"

"It's not safe for me anywhere, and I've a task I must complete."

The witch rose as Drest skittered toward the door. "Wait—Drest!"

But Drest ducked outside before Merewen could catch her again.

⊷ 17 ⊶

THE KEEP

D rest pushed through the crowded bailey toward the castle's keep, her hood up. A handful of men in green surcoats emblazoned with white hawks wandered about, but there were twice as many Faintree Castle knights.

Something was wrong.

Drest slipped to the edge of the crowd, away from the knights. From there, she strode up to the keep. Its pattern of mortar and stone made a perfect surface for climbing, but she merely walked alongside it.

A servant in a drab brown tunic was emptying a pot of dirty water into the grass. Drest fell into step behind him as he returned to the doors. She kept her head down, though from the corner of her eye she was aware of the shapes around her. A page in green and blue. A barefoot girl. A Harkniss knight—and then she was at the doors, two slabs of oak studded with iron nails, then past them.

The chamber she entered was huge, reeking of damp hay and sweat. Green rushes crunched underfoot, lit by the windows set high upon the tapestry-covered walls.

Four Faintree Castle knights in full armor marched by, followed by a cluster of young men wearing azure blue and black. She skittered away from them, past servants in green tunics and blue hose, to the wall.

If this castle was like Emerick's, the lady would be upstairs, in a fine chamber. But where?

Drest darted to the nearest stairway and took the steps quickly. She slipped past servant after servant on her way up, men and women carrying jugs, trays, and linens.

The stairway twisted and grew narrow. Was this the way? She was beginning to wonder when she came around a curve and bumped into a young woman carrying a basket of fragrant bread.

"I beg your pardon!" The woman laughed. "A bit tight in here, eh? Are you looking for something?"

"Aye," said Drest. "Do you know where Lady de Moys is? I need to speak to her." She hesitated, then went on in a rush: "I know it's not the day she sees people, but I need to see her today. It's important. I'm one of her allies—I mean, my friend is—I mean—he needs her—and he's too scared to come inside himself, so I have his message for her."

The young woman's smile had disappeared at the start of Drest's words, but her face had softened by the end. "I can understand that; a castle *is* a scary place. You're a brave soul to search by yourself like this. Come, I'll show you where the lady is and you can give her your friend's message."

She led Drest upstairs, past more halls, then down a hall that led to another stairway. Drest kept to the young woman's heels. At last, they stopped on a landing.

"Here you are. Knock, then announce yourself. Good luck to you, dear."

"Thank you," said Drest as the woman went back down the stairs.

Swallowing, Drest knocked on the nail-studded door, then pushed it open.

The wood scraped against the stone, revealing a wide room rich with purple and yellow tapestries—and a woman sitting at a table piled high with parchments.

The woman stood. She was as tall as Emerick and wore a rich burgundy gown with a dark green mantle. Her face, surrounded by a short white veil, was cold and stern.

"I've asked to be alone. Who let you in?"

The lady's castle voice was like a lash.

⤜ 18 ⤛

LADY DE MOYS

Slowly, Drest pushed shut the door behind her. "I need your help."

Lady de Moys's eyes narrowed. "Who are you?"

Everything seemed to waver before Drest. "My name is Drest. Aye, like the bloodthirsty Picts. I cannot say who my father is; Emerick would not want me to."

Astonishment made the lady, for that instant, seem young. "*Who?* You cannot mean—"

"Aye," said Drest, "it's who you think: Emerick Faintree. I know him. He asked me to find you and beg for your help."

Lady de Moys's face turned cold again. "Lord Faintree is dead. Why do you come here with a lie?"

"I'm not lying." Drest's fingers itched for Tancored, but she kept them loose at her side. "He's really here, in your bailey, and he's afraid to come up because—" She swallowed. "If you don't listen, I'll never—he'll never—"

"What are you talking about? Why are you here?"

Drest took a deep breath. "Emerick Faintree is my greatest friend, and he's hunted, and wounded. He cannot keep running, but if he doesn't, he'll die."

The lady shook her head. "If he's alive, you're speaking to the wrong person. His uncle is amassing armies to find and slay the villains who murdered him. I have given Sir Oswyn my own army, and he's sent them to the western borders. If you speak the truth, go find Oswyn and tell *him* this story."

A cold realization filled Drest. Oswyn had known they'd beg help from Lady de Moys, Emerick's only ally. So he'd taken her army for himself.

He's a clever devil. Her father's voice boomed in her mind. *He's tearing every support from around the lord to make sure he falls.*

Drest's fingers traced Tancored's grip. "You've been lied to, lady. *Oswyn's* the one hunting Emerick, not my da. Oswyn would be glad to have a dagger stuck in Emerick's ribs; then he'll have that lordship for himself. Did you not know that?"

Understanding washed over Lady de Moys's face. "*You* are the bloodthirsty lass I've heard about, the one Oswyn saw in the chamber window murdering poor Emerick!" She crossed her arms. "Get out of this room!"

"Nay! I was in Emerick's chamber *rescuing* him,"

snapped Drest. "His uncle had sent Sir Maldred up to slay him and—"

"His uncle had sent Sir Maldred up to *protect* him—from *you*!" The lady strode toward the door. "I never admired Maldred, but I would not call him a traitor."

"He's not just a traitor; he's a murderer. He's the one who slew the lady Celestria and said it'd been my da. She was trying to escape. She was fleeing her betrothal with Lord de Moys."

Lady de Moys froze at the door, her hand upon the iron ring. "You take a great risk coming here with a price on your head. What did you possibly think you'd gain from me?"

"I want your help, like I said." A sob rose in Drest's throat. "I want your army to take back Faintree Castle. I want to go there and be safe. I want—nay, this isn't about me, but Emerick, for he needs to be the lord again at his castle, and I swear he's alive and in your bailey now, hiding from his knights."

Slowly, the lady turned around. "How did you know that Celestria had been betrothed to my husband first?"

"Emerick told me."

"What else do you know of Celestria? Prove that what you've said is true."

Drest took a deep breath and tried to think back. What

had her friend told her about his sister? "Emerick—he told me that Celestria loved my da. He was the only man-at-arms who listened to her. The only one who cared about her."

She wasn't allowed to talk to him, whispered Emerick's voice, *but still she did.*

"She wasn't allowed to talk with the men-at-arms," Drest faltered, "but she'd meet him on the castle grounds anyway. Celestria must have been very strong to do that against her father's orders. From all Emerick's said, it sounds like he was a brute."

A line twitched in the lady's cheek. "He was. Go on."

Oriana was her greatest friend—

"You were her friend, were you not? Did she tell you that she was writing to my da to ask him to rescue her from that marriage?"

"I knew." Her voice was like the whisper of wind.

Drest hesitated. "Emerick didn't know what had happened that night until my da told him. My da tried to rescue her. But the old lord's knights came and—and she rushed up to stop them from slaying my da. That's when Sir Maldred slew her. Maldred escaped, but Da slew the other knights in his rage. He could not bear it. She was his wee lady, see, and he hadn't saved her."

A gasp came from Lady de Moys. She put a shaking

hand over her mouth. "Celestria—she said that's what he always called her: 'my wee lady.' Did your father tell you what *she* called *him*? 'My truest knight.' "

"Nay, I never heard that. I don't think he felt like that after she died."

Lady de Moys walked slowly to the other side of the room.

Drest shifted from foot to foot. "Da said he'll always serve Emerick because they both loved Lady Celestria. And I'll always help Emerick because he's my greatest friend in all the world, and I will die for him if I must."

"So he has a friend at last."

The lady began to walk back. When she reached Drest, her face was fierce and resolute.

"I will crush Sir Oswyn into *dust*," Lady de Moys snarled. "I do not brook liars or traitors, and those who betray me pay dearly for it."

The fury in her voice was like the crashing of a violent tide.

"Meet me at Faintree Castle. I'll send Sir Peter, my most trusted man, to fetch my army from the west. If he rides swiftly, he'll catch my men before they've advanced all the way, and they can be at Faintree in three days. And then I shall lead the twenty-five knights whom Oswyn left here under the guise of friendship toward their own castle.

There they shall meet *my* knights. Can you be at Faintree Castle in three days?"

Drest straightened. "Aye, lady."

"Take care with that price on your head. That's three days you'll need to hide." Her gaze softened, until it was almost gentle. "You are very good to Emerick, and very determined, to come here like this. I can see why Oswyn fears you."

The lady held out her hand.

Drest stared. Was she to take it? Kiss it? She didn't know, and so she took it and gripped it as she would have one of her brothers'.

The lady's fingers closed tightly over Drest's. She raised their clasped hands.

"You will stay strong. And brave, and bold. You will live beyond this curse, and rise to glory. I say this, so shall it be."

With a smile at last, though it was a faint, hard smile, Lady de Moys leaned over Drest and kissed her forehead.

"Now go." She released Drest's hand.

Footsteps pounded in the hallway outside, and a shout echoed at the door.

Drest threw back her cloak and drew Tancored with a swish.

"Lady de Moys!" Someone pounded on the wood. "My lady!"

"Stand out of sight, against the wall," she whispered, and waited for Drest to dart behind her. Then she pulled the door open.

"My lady!" cried a man in the hallway. "There is a thief and imposter loose in the castle. He's stolen the helm and tunic of one of our guards. Do you wish me to bring men to watch before your door?"

"Thank you, Sir William, but no: I'll keep my door shut and barred. And Sir William—if you find that thief and imposter, bring him to me. Do not let the Faintree knights meddle in this."

"Yes, my lady."

Footsteps—and the knight was gone.

Lady de Moys drew the door shut. "A stolen helm and tunic. I wonder who that could be."

"It's not Emerick; he's hiding by the tannery."

"I pray you're right. Now put away your sword and go. It will not be safe for you on the stairs with the Faintree knights helping with the search, but I shall tell you another way outside."

Drest sheathed her weapon.

"Listen closely: Go fifteen steps down the stairs from this door and hunt for a panel on the left with a faint hand-print in the stone. Push the handprint. Enter where it opens. Go down the path within, keeping to your right. It will be dark, but if your hand remains on the wall, it will guide you to the end, where you'll find an opening in the kitchen. Beg for a bite, but don't linger. Go into the bailey and find Emerick, and take him through the gates as quickly as you can. Remember: fifteen steps."

"Fifteen," Drest repeated.

The lady's cold eyes bored into hers. "When you see Emerick, tell him not to fear. He must try to be as strong as you." Lady de Moys pulled open the door. "Now go."

Drest bowed and dashed into the hall.

⸙ 19 ⸙

THE PASSAGEWAY

Drest ran down the stairs—but in seconds, stopped. She'd forgotten to start counting.

How could you forget to count, you rat-faced boar? moaned Uwen's voice.

"Nay, I'll just find it," muttered Drest. She skittered down a few steps, searching for the handprint.

The thundering of castle men's boots came from the stairs below.

"Not here, not here, not—" She broke off: A small handprint was faintly visible in the chunk of stone on the step below her, a carving light with age.

Drest set her hand against it and pushed.

The stone did not move.

Push harder, lass! Thorkill's voice.

The castle men's footsteps were closer.

Drest threw all her weight into her next push.

The stone slid into the wall, then past into an empty space beyond.

She scrambled through the opening, into darkness, and shoved the stone back into the wall.

One second. Two.

Footsteps pounded past on the other side. Drest waited, her hands on the stone. She would be ready to hold it firm against any knight who tried to push through.

But the stone did not move.

Drest sat back. Her shoulders were tight with tension, her breath caught in her chest. Worst of all, the dark was absolute, weighing on her eyes like the sea.

Calm down. Gobin's voice. *You're here in the passageway. You're safe.*

Footsteps clicked. Inside the passage.

Close, as if someone had been waiting in the darkness.

Drest fumbled with her tunic and silently drew her dagger.

A boot scraped on stone not more than three feet away. A hand, large and firm, closed on Drest's leg.

"That's you, Drest, is it not?" It was Emerick's voice.

She'd almost stabbed him. Quickly, she slid her dagger back into its sheath, then followed his hand up his arm to his shoulder, over a collar of chain mail, and flung her arm around his neck.

"You're the greatest crab-headed fool who ever lived! Did you not trust me?"

His arm closed tightly around her. "I saw Sir Roland confront you. I felt like such a coward. You escaped that time, but what if someone saw you, and guessed who you were? I had to follow you." He gave an uncertain laugh. "So I stole a helm and uniform of a man-at-arms who was bathing in the river. He didn't notice at first, but then he started shouting. I had to hide. Then I saw *you* go into the keep—"

Drest hung on to him for a few seconds longer, then let him go.

"I'm sorry," Emerick said miserably. "I shouldn't have stolen these. I should have simply crept in as myself. Now we must either make a run for the solar to find Oriana, or a run for our way out. They're hunting for the thief, you see."

"We can find our way out. I met with the lady."

Emerick seized her leg again. "You did? Did she listen? Did she believe you?"

"Aye," began Drest, "but—"

"Well done! And her army? Will she lend me her men? Can we go back to her and have her summon them?"

"Aye, she'll lend us her men, but she needs three days to fetch them. Emerick—Oswyn tricked her into sending her army to the west."

"God's *bones*," Emerick moaned. "He's stolen my only ally!"

Drest gripped Emerick's shoulder. "But she's still *your* ally, and she'll never be *his* again. Lad, it's only three days. And we'll meet at your castle."

A new pounding of feet came from outside the stone.

"I know, I know," Emerick said when the sound had died, "but three more days of running and hiding—can you manage it, Drest? It seems as if deadly peril faces you wherever we turn."

"I'm good with deadly peril, am I not?" She patted his shoulder. "Where's your hand? Let's find the kitchen and fetch supplies for our journey."

His fingers clasped hers, and the two began to scramble down the dark path.

But Emerick stopped abruptly.

Drest bumped up behind him. She was about to ask what was wrong, but then she heard it too:

The sound of clinking, mail-covered footsteps. They were within the passageway ahead.

◂ 20 ▸

THE CHASE

Emerick leaned back until his cheek was touching her hair. "There's another path. It branches off below."

"No talking," Drest whispered. "Just find it."

Emerick crept along. Drest padded after him, her right hand on his belt. With her left, she drew her dagger.

If they met the unseen knight—and it *had* to be a knight with that clink of chain mail boots—she would have just enough room to pull Emerick back and lunge forward in his place.

Clink. Clink. The steps were moving faster. The knight was no longer trying to be quiet.

The dagger's grip was slippery in Drest's sweating hand.

And then—Emerick stumbled. There was a drop, and he was sliding into it.

Drest clamped her dagger's grip between her teeth and grabbed Emerick with both hands, one on his belt, the other on a chunk of his stolen tunic. This was something Wulfric had taught her—how to pull Uwen up from a cliff if he fell.

Use your knees and not your back to lift him, lass, boomed Wulfric's voice.

But Emerick had slipped too much, and she was on her knees. With a grunt, Drest pulled, using all her weight to drag him back onto the path.

He lay there, panting.

"I know where we are," Emerick whispered. "The passage we want is just before us, beyond the drop. God's bones, I almost plummeted to my death there."

Drest took the dagger from her jaws. "Show me the passage."

Emerick crawled forward. The ledge became narrow and the walls tight. Drest bade herself think only of the muddy heels she held and not of the footsteps that were running now.

The passage became a slope, and the slope became stairs inside a new narrow passage.

Drest sprang to her feet and pulled Emerick up.

"This is the way," he murmured. "It's very tight here—it always has been—but with any luck—"

"Keep going!"

The steps went down. And soon the two were running, stumbling, holding the walls to keep on their feet.

Behind them, there was a scrape. A deep voice swore.

The stairway curved and split into two. Emerick followed the one on the left—which became another passage, straight and long. Now they ran freely.

Suddenly, Emerick halted.

"This is it. The way out. Here, Drest, help me push this stone. It's a drop, not too high, onto grass—" He paused. "Wait. I've thought of something. You'll be noticed when we jump. Oh, God, they'll see a lass with a sword and they'll know—"

Drest grabbed Emerick's arm. "Aye, I *will* have my sword, and I'll draw it as soon as we hit the ground. They'll be afraid of this wolf's head when they see me. And then we'll run to the curtain wall. You can climb a wall, can't you?"

He was quiet.

"You *will* climb that wall, Emerick. Are you ready? Where's the stone?"

She felt for his hands. They held hers for a moment, then guided them to the panel. Together, their hands side by side, they pushed.

The stone block scraped, jolted, and then it was out, sailing through the open air. Before it thumped on to the grass, Drest hooked her arm in Emerick's and leaped, pulling him with her.

The sky was blindingly bright, and at first Drest could not see. It wasn't a high drop, but she hit the ground awkwardly. She was on her feet in seconds, though, her hand on her sword. Beside her, Emerick was struggling to rise.

Two guards on the other side of the green were racing toward them.

Drest's fingers closed over Tancored's grip. Any one of her brothers would have drawn his sword and stood ready to fight.

But Gobin's voice murmured deep in her mind:

What do you do best, lass? Run. So run while you still can.

She let Tancored go and hauled Emerick to his feet. He crumpled, his weight upon her. Drest threw his arm over her shoulder, looped her arm around his waist, and started sprinting toward the curtain wall.

AT THE CURTAIN WALL

The field was open, its grass cropped short by grazing sheep, but brown flashed everywhere on the bailey: the guards.

Drest focused on the towering curtain wall ahead. She tried to fly as she had always flown on the headland, but Emerick's weight slowed her. The fall had harmed him; he was leaning heavily, as he had in the days of their journey when his rib wound had plagued him most.

"Almost there," panted Drest.

Almost there, but now there were four guards—and a splash of blue on white ran alongside them.

Drest's boots pounded on the grass, her desperate energy keeping them ahead.

At last they were at the curtain wall, a shadowy stone giant covered with cracks, sprigs of moss, and crumbling mortar.

Drest propped Emerick up. "Start climbing!"

He pressed his pale, pain-clenched face against the wall. "I can't climb."

"I'll be right behind you. Start climbing, quick!"

"Go, Drest. Save your own life. I'll hold them back." He cast a frantic, hopeless glance at her. "I can't climb walls. Even when I'm well. I don't know how."

All feeling rushed out of Drest.

Emerick's pale blue eyes fixed on her in despair.

"*Why* did no one teach you to climb a wall?" she bellowed.

But she knew that shouting would do no good against the guards and knight who were closing in on them. She stepped away from Emerick and drew her sword.

"Drest, I—I order you to go," he stammered.

The lowering sun lit the steel. Tancored's weight seemed to thrum up her arm, through her body, and to her heart.

She settled herself into a fighting position: one foot forward, the other to the side, knees bent, ready to pivot.

All her years of training had prepared her for this moment. Drest took a deep breath.

A bleating cry pierced the air.

A sheep ran wildly past them as if buffeted on a wave.

Another sheep called out, running just as fast. Then another. A chorus of deafening bleats.

Drest stared. A flock of sheep was flooding the grounds, pooling frantically around the guards.

"Get out of the way!" shouted the Faintree Castle knight, but the sheep only pressed closer.

Sheep are not easily stirred, said Thorkill's voice. *Someone's alarmed them.*

Tig? Drest's heart lifted. Using animals instead of weapons—that was like him.

But a tall, cloaked figure—not Tig—was weaving among the sheep. It was a woman, and she veered to the wall and dashed alongside it toward them. Her cap slid off in her rush. A wave of gray hair streamed in her wake as she drew near.

Merewen.

Her silver falcon's eyes were wild. "Sheathe your sword and I shall help you," she gasped. "Hurry, child!"

"I won't leave Emerick—"

"Why do you think I am here?" She darted around Drest to Emerick's side and pulled him to his feet. "Listen to me, lord: I shall kneel, and you shall climb upon my shoulders. Drest—climb first and grasp his hands from above so that I can rise, and from there you will take him. Do you understand?"

It was a method of climbing that Grimbol had made the lads practice: a means to help an injured brother.

Drest sheathed her sword, thrust her fingers into the wall's cracks, and scrambled up.

The crumbling mortar gave her many easy holds. Within seconds, she was at the top, a wide surface pitted with stone battlements. She slipped between the merlons, hooked her feet on the other side, and turned and reached down.

"You can't be serious," Emerick murmured.

"You are risking the lives of us all, lord," snapped Merewen. "Make haste!"

With a muted sob, he stumbled to the wall. Gripping the ridges between the stones, he stepped onto the witch's shoulders.

"Hold yourself steady," said Merewen.

Drest reached down, stretching as far as she could. Emerick's shaking hand rose. Their fingertips brushed.

Not close enough.

She slipped a foot free from its hold on the other side of the battlement and stretched again—and this time, touched his hand. Praying that her one foot's hold would be strong, Drest seized his hand, and pulled.

That pull took a fraction of weight from Merewen's shoulders. Bracing herself against the stone wall, she slowly stood, lifting Emerick just a little—

Drest's hand closed over his wrist, then his forearm, then his elbow.

She crawled back on the battlement, pulling him toward

her, until he was close enough to grab the nearest merlon and drag himself into the crenel.

Drest seized his legs and, scrambling over them, thrust them to the other side. "We'll have to slide. Merewen?" She hooked her feet onto the battlement again and reached down.

The river of sheep was now mostly at the far end of the bailey, tangling the guards who were streaming from there. The other guards were running free.

"Merewen! Grab my hand!"

The witch stepped away from the wall. "No, child. Move swiftly. Help him down, and run. I shall keep them back."

"But Merewen—"

"Do what I say," roared the witch in a terrible voice, "and value your precious life for once! I will save myself!" She turned and set off into a run along the curtain wall.

"Drest! How do we get down?" Emerick was pulling at her.

She crawled back to his side.

"Hold on to my shoulders," she said, her throat hollow. "We're going to slide down, and we need to slow ourselves with our feet. Let me get under you. Are you ready?"

Panting, Emerick nodded and grabbed her shoulders. Drest slipped over the edge and down the wall.

Emerick's dragging feet made up for his weight. Soon

Drest's fingers were raw, but they quickly reached the ground.

Merewen.

But there was no time to see if she'd escaped.

Hoisting Emerick's arm over her shoulder, Drest dragged him running into the woods.

✦ 22 ✦

THE WARRIOR'S TASK

"You should have left me."

Emerick had not spoken for hours. They'd run, then plodded, then staggered along, and now their pace was simply limping. The sky was clear and the waning moon shed an unearthly brightness over the woods like shimmering water. All around them, branches hairy with twigs stood out like spirits in the mist.

"Nay, I did what was right," Drest said.

A tremble threatened her voice. She'd been thinking of Merewen, and of Tig, whose fates she did not know; and of her family, gone off beyond her reach. Worry about them all, not just the three days ahead, had seeped into her—but she wasn't about to show it.

"We escaped, did we not?" she went on gruffly. "Aye, and with the lady's promise, we'll be inside your castle soon. All we need to do is keep alive for three days. I've done well with today."

"But Merewen—do you think she escaped?"

"She might have."

"All those sheep," Emerick murmured. "She must have spooked them for us. I wonder if they helped *her* as well."

"They might have."

"You almost didn't escape. Because of me."

Drest halted. "Do you not want your castle back?"

"I do, but—"

"Do you not want to be a true lord again?"

"Yes, but Drest—"

"Sometimes people have to risk their lives. And sometimes people fall. Da always talked about the battles he'd fought along with your castle and the friends who'd fallen and how he'd grieved but knew he had to go on—"

"I don't want *any* of that castle if it means you'll risk your life at every opportunity." Emerick paused, breathing hard. "Drest, I do not take our friendship lightly. No one in this world matters more to me than you. If ever we should be in that situation again and *my* death would ensure *your* life, you must let me die for you."

In the distance, an owl hooted.

Drest pulled at her sword-belt. "You have to accept what I've risked for you if you want your castle back, and stop treating me like a wee lass. I'm a warrior like any of your knights. I *have* to take risks."

"I'm a warrior as well, Drest, and I've as much right as you to risk my life—"

"*You're* not a warrior! You're a lord, and *my* task—the warrior's task—is to keep you safe."

"But if the warrior has a price on her head—"

"Then it's my task to keep us *both* safe!"

"But—but Drest, that makes no sense!"

They stood apart, glowering at each other.

Emerick's shoulders slumped.

She drifted back to his side. "How are your wounds?"

"I feel horrible. Every part of me aches. You?"

"I feel like running."

"*Running?*"

"Aye, but I always feel like running when I'm edgy. Shall we find a place to sleep instead?"

Together, they searched for a spot and soon found a damp hollow beneath a sprawling clump of juniper branches.

The soil was soft, and Emerick sank into it gratefully. Drest crawled after him and drew her cloak over them both, a blanket of green wool.

It was thick, very much like the black wool cloak that had shielded them on their last journey.

The cloak that Merewen had given her.

Drest's eyes stung.

She wanted to save my life. She asked me to go with her. And when I refused, she risked her own life to save mine.

You risked your life to save hers once, said Gobin's voice, *so this is but a return of the favor.*

Nay, Drest thought, *it's not the same.*

She burrowed against Emerick and tried to hear only the slow, steady rhythm of his heart. She also tried to conjure the memory of Elys's hand again, but it didn't come that night.

Something warm, soft, and itchy rubbed against Drest's face. She shook her head, and sat up. Her mouth tasted of feathers.

Caa!

A glossy black crow hopped back, out of the juniper branches, and cocked its head to glare at Drest.

"Mordag?" Drest crawled free and soon was inches from the crow.

Caa.

Right to her face.

Drest called into the tangle, "Emerick? Look, it's Mordag!"

He dragged himself out with more speed that she had expected a wounded man could manage.

"Mordag." Emerick reached out a shaking hand toward the bird. "Is it really you? God bless you if it is. Where's your lad? Where's Tig?"

The crow let out a croak, then flapped hard and was in the air and next on a branch above their heads, a solid black shape against the rising sun.

"Show us," Drest said. "Will you do that, lass? Show us Tig."

"Don't do anything rash," Emerick warned.

Mordag hopped to another branch, then another, and then was flitting between the trees.

Drest crept with her habitual silence after the crow, steadying Emerick when he stumbled, never letting go of his hand.

Mordag flapped ahead, out of sight, and gave a sharp call.

Drest pulled up short. "That's the call for enemies," she whispered. "They must be straight ahead."

"Don't rush in." Emerick squeezed her hand. "Don't— just *don't*, please."

"Nay, I won't, but if Tig's there and needs my help—"

A voice cut through her next word—a man's voice, rich and low.

"What do you think *that* means?"

It was a castle voice, one that Drest had never heard.

⟵ 23 ⟶

LOYAL MEN

Mordag called again, the same sharp, piercing noise. But then she flew back and landed on a branch over Drest's head. From there, she gave another call, the softer *caa* that she had directed toward Drest as she woke.

"And what of that one?" said the castle voice. "Do you know?"

"I do, in fact," said a laughing voice that made Drest's heart race.

It was Tig.

"But I can't tell you *that* one," Tig went on. "The first meant 'enemy.' I hope you'll pardon her."

"Yes, of course I'll take no offense."

"May I see where she is? I'll keep within sight."

The castle voice laughed. "Why do I have the sense that you could duck out of sight in this very clearing, and none of us would know where you went? Do what you must, lad."

Silence.

And then the branches were moving, and Tig—his clothes streaked with mud and dirt, his hair full of tangles—was before them.

A grin as bright as sunshine on the sea lit his face. "I thought it might be you."

Before Drest had a chance to grab and hug him, Tig had his arms around her, then around Emerick.

"I can't believe that you're both here," Tig said. "I kept sending Mordag out to search for you, but—but that's a bit much even for her."

"What happened to you?" Emerick whispered. "Who were you talking with back there? We thought you were going to Phearsham Ridge for supplies and had been delayed or caught—"

"You're not safe, are you," Drest interrupted. "Shall we take you away?"

Tig's arm tightened around her shoulder. "I *am* safe, if you can believe it, and not just because *you're* standing here. Yes, Emerick, I went back to the village, and yes, I did pack supplies. That man—Sir Fergal—had left, and everyone was tense." Tig's eyes sparkled. "Guess who I met as I was staggering out the back door in the dark with our supplies? Four knights and eight men-at-arms—*and* Sir Fergal.

I thought my heart was going to drop out of my chest, I was so frightened."

"Oh, Tig," Drest whispered. "Did they catch you?"

"Indeed they did. Sir Fergal—that man is as slimy as a slug—he pointed at me and said I knew where the blood-thirsty lass who had murdered Lord Faintree was hiding. So they took off my bag of supplies and hauled me away, bound by my wrists. Drest, you were right: There *are* bands of knights with squires and men-at-arms prowling the woods and road for you. This band is larger than usual because the man who leads it is important."

Emerick pointed at Tig's hands. "But you're not bound any longer. And just now—that man sounded like Sir Reynard, of all people, the leader of my army. But it can't be; he never leaves the castle except for wars."

"Well, he left your castle for something else this time: to hunt for your murderer. Yes, it's Sir Reynard back there. And the reason that I'm like this"—he held up his hands, apart—"instead of this"—he pressed his wrists together—"is that Sir Reynard is a good, kind, reasonable man who listens."

Emerick smiled.

"None of them fully believed me, except for Sir Reynard, so I led him back to the place where we rested. If it wasn't for your footprint, Emerick—I found one in the moss by the tree, sunk deep where you were limping—I don't think they'd have followed me. But they believed me when I said it was yours, and I've been leading them through the woods, pointing out your footprints where I can." Tig laughed again. "It's remarkable, really, if you think about it: Five knights, four squires, and eight men-at-arms following *me*, of all people, through the woods on a wild chase."

"If Sir Reynard believes you, the rest have no choice but to follow." Emerick glanced at the trees behind Tig. "Are they all back there? Tig, are they loyal, or—or will they try to slay Drest? Or me?"

"Everyone's loyal. Yes, including Sir Fergal, who seems swayed by the others. So don't worry, Emerick; these are good knights, ones you can trust. Come with me. You'll be among your faithful men again. And Drest." He faced her. "You're safe now."

Emerick was beaming, and hugged Drest tightly.

She let him, but did not hug him back.

Emerick would be safe. Tig had secured him a group of loyal knights, and they would fight for him as much as she would.

And yet knights—she had not met many who hadn't tried to slay or capture her.

Suddenly, the branches before them moved. A knight,

brown-skinned and old, his chain mail hood down to reveal his thick gray hair, appeared.

Tig pivoted neatly to face him, and bowed. "As you can see, Sir Reynard, I wasn't lying."

But the knight was not looking at Tig. His eyes were fixed on Emerick alone. Dark eyes that abruptly filled with tears.

"My lord," said the knight, and lunged forward—

—to throw himself to his knees before Emerick. He grabbed the young lord's hand and held it in his own against his bowing forehead.

"You—you don't have to do that," stammered Emerick.

The knight pushed his other hand against the ground and grunted as he rose. "Where are you wounded, my lord? Tig said you'd been badly hurt."

"On my ribs. And my shoulder. It was Maldred. Did Tig tell you? He came into the solar with his sword, and Drest—" Now Emerick was pulling her forward, forcing her before the knight. "Reynard, this is Grimbol's daughter. She's not a bloodthirsty lass but the hero who saved my life and—and she's my greatest friend. There's a hideous sentence upon her head. She deserves not it but the highest honor the castle can give."

Sir Reynard's eyes flicked over her.

Her hand was ready to dive into her tunic for her dagger.

"Drest, I swear that I am as loyal to Lord Faintree as you are. You will be safe, and honored, among my men." He gestured back at the trees. "Come. We have a camp set up. And it would make the men very, *very* pleased to see proof that Tig's tales are true."

They followed Tig and Sir Reynard back between the trees. The old knight held the branches aside for them. His gaze sought Emerick, and a tender smile flitted upon his lips. It was the kind of smile that Grimbol had always given Drest.

Men-at-arms—eight, as Tig had said—were sitting throughout the clearing, mending, knotting, sharpening. And there were four knights. Four young men in azure and black sat with them.

All of them stopped their tasks to stare at Emerick. And then they rose, bolting toward him to fall upon their knees, heads bowed.

Emerick swallowed.

"His lordship has been injured, as Tig said." Sir Reynard seemed about to say more, but paused and pointed to one of the boys. "Frery, fetch his lordship a cloak and some rations—"

"*That's* the bloodthirsty lass."

143

It was a murmur that nonetheless cut through Sir Reynard's words.

The knight who had spoken slowly stood.

A domed forehead, thinning hair, a long jaw, and piercing dark eyes—

Drest drew in her breath.

It was Sir Fergal.

⊰ 24 ⊱

NOT EVERY ONE

Within seconds, her dagger was in her hand.

The castle men rose to their feet. Scrapes of steel against leather—blades leaving scabbards—filled the clearing as they drew their weapons.

But then Sir Reynard's voice rang out: "Her name is Drest. She's Grimbol's daughter but also Lord Faintree's guard and friend. Now fetch *her* some rations too."

No one moved.

"Drest is to be honored among you all," said Emerick coldly. "Anyone who touches her will be slain on the spot."

Slowly, the men sheathed their weapons.

Sir Fergal was the last.

"Did you hear me, Sir Fergal?" Emerick snapped.

The knight swiftly bowed. "Yes, of course, my lord. I would not *think* of harming your friend, now that I know what she is." He sat down in his spot by the edge of the trees.

Soon Emerick was settled among his men, cloaks wrapped around him, Sir Reynard at his side.

Tig drew Drest away from them to the corner of the clearing. "Tell me where you've been."

Drest leaned against a tree and took a bite of the hearth bread and cheese that one of the squires had given her. "To Harkniss Castle. The lady's meeting us at Faintree in three days. Tig, that Sir Fergal is watching me."

The boy twisted around. "And Mordag is watching *him*. Don't you trust her?"

The crow was perched directly above the knight, who averted his eyes from Drest's stare.

"Aye, I trust your crow, but—lad, I don't trust knights." She took another bite from her bread, though she could barely taste it. "There's thirty pounds on my head. Do you think Sir Fergal won't try to get it?"

"Emerick just gave an order, and Sir Fergal's not about to defy him. Knights don't disobey direct orders—"

"How can you be sure? Aye, it's one order, but Sir Oswyn gave him another, and there's thirty pounds in *his*—"

"Drest, calm down. No one's going to hurt you."

A few of the castle men who were clustered around Emerick glanced over.

Tig stepped between them and Drest, blocking their view. "Please. You could have no better guard than the people around you now. If you trust me at all, you'll believe me."

Drest set her hand on Tancored's pommel and squeezed

hard. "I trust you, lad, but these knights—and that man—and those thirty pounds—"

Tig looked away, his jaw tight.

He risked his life for you with these knights, you know, murmured Gobin's voice. *He could have tricked them and run off. But he didn't. For you.*

Drest seized Tig's hand. "I'm sorry. I'm jumpy. I can't help it."

"Will you feel better if we join the knights? They're not bad people. And you have to get used to them if you're going to live at Faintree Castle."

Hand in hand, they approached Emerick's seat. He was telling the story of what had happened since he had arrived on the headland with Sir Maldred and his men, his voice the haughty castle voice of those days. He had slipped back into it with ease.

"—and it was a miracle indeed that I had made it that far. It was then that we encountered the bandit again—ah, Drest. Come sit with us."

Men moved aside, making room. She sank to a crouch next to Emerick's mound of cloaks.

Emerick reached down and took her hand. "All of you, look closely at this lass. I want you to know Drest. I owe her my life. I cannot tell you how many times she's saved me at the risk of—of *everything*. Even just now, at Harkniss

Castle, she went inside by herself—and—God's bones, she's truly my greatest friend who ever—she—" His voice wavered, and broke.

"You are exerting yourself too much, my lord," Sir Reynard said gently. "You've come all the way from Harkniss in that state. Please rest. And know that we will honor and protect this lass for her great, great service to you."

With her eyes lowered, she leaned against Emerick's leg.

"My lord, let me tell you what you'll be facing." Sir Reynard's voice became hard and regal. "Oswyn has sent warbands of knights and men-at-arms to hunt for Drest and her father—and, it seems, for you. He has seventy-five men with him, and has left fifty to guard the castle—"

"Why were *you* not left at the castle, Reynard?" interrupted Emerick.

"Because Oswyn told me to comb these woods for the Mad Wolf's lass; he said he'd seen her on the headland. The twenty-five knights at Harkniss are to join me by the week's end and comb the woods again." Sir Reynard's eyes flicked to Drest. "Quite a fuss, you might think, but you're his greatest enemy."

On the other side of the camp. Mordag let out a hoarse call.

Emerick squeezed Drest's hand. "That's a distinction you should be proud of."

"That's a distinction that I had not fully understood until I heard what you said, Lord Faintree." Sir Reynard gave a grim smile. "Of course she'd be his nightmare: She'd stopped the slayings he attempted, of both her family and of you. He's not about to forgive that." His face lightened. "You're really quite extraordinary, Drest."

"Nay, I just do what I must," she murmured. Slowly, she raised her eyes.

All the castle men were watching her. But they were smiling at her too.

Sir Reynard cleared his throat. "My lord, we shall have to think how to amass your army and capture Oswyn soon. If we can do that before he returns to Faintree Castle, you'll have no trouble gaining back all your men. But if he gets there first, they'll not believe you're alive, and will side with him. I suggest we fetch the twenty-five from Harkniss, borrow horses, and set up a blockade upon the road."

"You won't need to go to Harkniss; they'll be coming with Lady de Moys in three days. She's lending me her army, you see, and they're meeting me at Faintree Castle."

Sir Reynard's eyes widened. "That's what you were doing at Harkniss? Well done, my lord."

"It was Drest's doing, actually—"

"Sir Reynard!" called one of the men at the far end of the clearing.

"Yes, Mal?"

"It's Sir Fergal, sir. He's gone."

Drest sprang to her feet.

The spot where the knight had been sitting was empty.

Mordag uttered a disgruntled cry.

"No," whispered Tig. "Mordag called before, and I wasn't listening. Drest—I'm sorry."

But she barely heard him. The traitorous knight who wanted her head had left his war-band. And he would be on the hunt for her again.

TO PHEARSHAM RIDGE

Sir Reynard sent four men after Sir Fergal, but they came back empty-handed. He had slipped away and disappeared, as if he were a creature of the trees.

At Emerick's request, the whole party hastened toward Phearsham Ridge, the nearest village. They could get supplies and healing salve and could hide until it was time to meet Lady de Moys at Faintree Castle. Tig and half the men led the group with Mordag swooping ahead. The rest of the men and the squires took up the rear. Drest and Sir Reynard marched on either side of the young lord.

Drest supported Emerick in the old manner. He clung to her shoulders as if he could not let go.

"Oswyn is playing a brutal game with us." Sir Reynard, who had been silent for much of the march, now spoke. "I've been thinking, Emerick—"

Strange, Drest thought. *He calls him by his name when they're alone. Was that a slip?*

Or affection? mused Nutkin. *He has a few strong friends at the castle, it seems.*

"—of what you said. And of what I know. No one even *suspected* that you were alive. He's wanted the lordship all his life, you understand."

"Yes, I realize that." Emerick's voice was sharp. "I'm surprised he didn't ask Grimbol to help him get it years ago."

A smile tweaked the corner of Sir Reynard's mouth. "Ah, but Grimbol was faithful to Lady Celestria more than anyone else. If she'd asked him to slay your father—or Oswyn—I wager he'd have done it, and a whole army of men-at-arms would have followed him. That must be why Oswyn had her murdered, and him charged for it. Both she—and he—were too powerful."

Emerick shivered.

"But now *you're* powerful with Grimbol serving you." Sir Reynard laughed. "That will surprise all your men. I shall have to think of what I'll say to him when I meet him next. I fear I wasn't polite when Maldred hauled him and his war-band into the castle last week." He leaned forward and met Drest's eyes. "By the by, I've been wondering: How did you escape our prison? Is there a weakness to that chamber that no one's noticed?"

"Nay, there's no weakness." She glanced at Emerick, whose lips were pinched in his attempt to hold back a smile.

"You were bound, were you not?"

"Aye, to an iron ring in the wall. Like my brothers and Da."

Sir Reynard waited. "What did you do?"

Drest shrugged. "I hung there. It felt as if my arms were going to tear off from my body thanks to my weight. And when it was too much, I climbed up, took off the rope, pushed aside the bolt of the trap, and climbed out."

"But—you were bound to an iron ring, and the bolt of the trap was on the *outside*, above your head—" Sir Reynard broke off. "Who helped you?"

"Why did someone have to help me? I did it on my own. I told you how. You may believe me or not."

"I'd believe her if I were you," Emerick said lightly.

"Bound to an iron ring, below a barred trapdoor." Sir Reynard shook his head. "No one else has escaped from that prison. Any who have freed themselves from the rope have fallen into the sea and drowned."

She met Emerick's eyes, and barely held in her grin. "Maybe they couldn't climb walls."

It was almost dusk, and they were nearly at the village. Through the trees in the distance, Drest saw Phearsham Ridge's golden wheat fields.

Ahead of them, Tig halted. He spoke a word to the knight at his side, then darted back between the men-at-arms to Drest.

"Do you smell that?" he said. "It's smoke."

She did. It was a drifting scent on the breeze, too pungent to be a bonfire or cook fire. It smelled as Soggyweald had after they had parted from Merewen there: like burning thatch.

All at once, Drest remembered her father's threat in the mill: If the farmers didn't protect Emerick while he was gone, he'd burn the village to the ground.

And he'd promised her he'd be back within five days—or sooner.

⤛ 26 ⤜

A VILLAGE ATTACKED

They ran toward Phearsham Ridge, toward the heavy stench of smoke. Soon they were at the barley and wheat fields, which were empty and silent.

"Men, ready yourselves," Sir Reynard ordered.

The three knights and all the men-at-arms drew their weapons.

Drest stood motionless. It would be like the headland— only worse. Her father and brothers did not have weapons, and would fall.

I can't let that happen.

She drew Tancored and stepped in front of the castle men. "I know what this is, and it's not for you to meet. It's for me."

"No, lass," Sir Reynard said. "It's not safe for you to enter a battle. Leave this to us."

"Nay, it's *my* battle. I can't tell you why, but—" She met Emerick's eyes, praying he'd know what she feared.

His eyes widened.

"—but I have to face this."

155

"I don't understand." Sir Reynard turned to Emerick. "What does this mean, my lord? Shall we advance?"

Emerick shook his head. "No, Drest is right. This is something that she and I must face. Lass, let's find Wimarca and ask how this happened. Tig, will you come with us?"

The boy was pale, but nodded.

"Why him?" snapped Sir Reynard. "Lord Faintree, you are taking your life far too lightly. *I'll* come with you and—"

"No, Reynard. Stay here by the fields. All of you. That is my order."

Drest and Tig rushed to Emerick's side, and they marched together into the darkening woods toward Wimarca's hut.

"Your father—" Emerick shook his head. "I cannot believe he would do this."

"He wouldn't, would he?" Tig cast Drest an anxious look.

"I don't know."

But she knew this: He must have returned to Phearsham Ridge uneasy with the farmers, and found both Emerick and her gone.

He'd burned other villages for less.

Soon they reached Wimarca's hut, where a horrible sight awaited.

The door was sprawled across the threshold, torn from its hinges. The healer's stool had been smashed into pieces, the kettle thrown across the room, and her table cleared of herbs and bowls. A sea of dried plants and broken pottery littered the floor. The bed had been slashed open and its contents—lady's bedstraw and swaths of homespun—had been thrown onto the cold fire circle.

There was no trace of Wimarca.

Tig spun around and sprinted toward the path to the mill.

Drest and Emerick followed, all three pounding through the woods up to the meadow.

The village was strangely hushed in that open space, and the scent of smoke was stronger. It grew dense and sickening as they advanced.

It was almost dark when they reached the top of the hill, where another grim sight met them.

Half the mill was gone, replaced by a blackened skeleton. The wheel was burned and crooked. But part of the house upon it remained, and wood had been propped up over the gaping holes, forming a fragile wall.

Tig let out a staggered breath. "No. *No.* Arnulf—Idony—"

He plunged on, up to the mill's back door. It was shut, but Tig shoved it open.

A knife flashed in the dim light from inside. The lad holding it stumbled away when he saw Tig.

The room was full of people.

Elys was there, pushing between the figures packed in the big room, past the lad, until she was at the door.

"Thank God you're safe!" She was outside then, and crushed Drest in her embrace.

"They're back!" called a man from inside.

A narrow path opened up between the villagers as they made way for Tig. Elys led Drest in, not letting go of her arm, and Emerick, and shut the door behind them.

All the villagers were there: the farmers, the old men and women; the village lads and lasses—

And Uwen and the twins, standing among the crowd.

And Wulfric and Thorkill, against the far wall.

And Grimbol, standing apart.

"What are you doing here?" Drest slipped away from Elys and up to her father. "Everything's burned! What have you done?"

Grimbol seized her shoulders roughly. "They said you'd gone! Into the woods, with no direction! Did you not hear my order?" He shook her, hard. "I leave you in this village to protect the lord, and what happens? You go on a wild run for no end but your own! Drest, you'll follow orders! I shall bind your arms and carry you on my back like a bairn if you won't!"

Drest tore herself free. "You're a *monster!* Da, why did you do this? Are you never done with your revenge?"

Rage filled Grimbol's eyes. It fit with the scars that ran deeper than the wrinkles on his face: white slashes over his eyebrow, jaw, and forehead. His voice lowered, and became threatening. "*What* did you just call me?"

The villagers were backing away.

But Wulfric was pushing through them.

"Wait, Da," he said. "Drest, what's this talk of revenge? Do you think *we* burned this village?"

Amazement wiped the fury from Grimbol's face.

Drest locked her jaw to keep it from shaking. "You told Wyneck you would, Da. I heard you say it, in this room."

Thorkill was pushing close, with Uwen at his heels, and then the twins, shoving the villagers, until Drest was surrounded by her brothers.

Each one of them was pale and streaked with ash. Part of Thorkill's tunic was singed, and a bleeding wound trailed down one side of Wulfric's face, near his eye to his chin.

"You think *we* did this?" Grimbol snapped. "Aye, we came back early because I did not feel right with you here alone, but this was not our doing. We came at night.

159

Wimarca told us you'd gone, running from a castle man, and we were up at the mill, readying to set off after you, when *they* came. Four knights: Hugh, James, Guy, and Aimo, all men from the lord's army, men I'd fought alongside years ago. But they were not here as friends. Without a sound, they slunk through this village lighting fires. Aye, but the first place they went was the healer's hut."

"Where is she?" Tig looked around frantically.

"Here. But only by the merest shred of luck." A figure wobbled to her feet near the empty hearth, swathed in blankets with a linen bandage around her head. "They asked me where the lord was, and when I did not tell them they destroyed my hut in anger. Uwen, lad?"

Uwen squeezed back through the crowd to Wimarca's side and grabbed her arm to hold her up. "Do you need me?"

"Oh, lad. What a question. Drest, your brother—he risked his life to save me. One of those men dragged me up to the burning mill, and thrust me in—"

"Your brother, lass, ran past him," said Hodge, whose manner was different now: respectful and humble. "He seemed not to feel the wind of that man's sword swinging at his back."

"He went into the fire to save her," said Torold, "while your brothers the twins—they stopped that knight."

Drest stared from Uwen to the twins. "You were fighting knights? Without swords?"

"We were *all* fighting knights, and aye, only Wulfric had a sword." Gobin's smile was faint. "Lass, don't be angry with Da; he ordered us to save the village."

"Drest, lass, what do you think we are?" Thorkill reached around her shoulders and held her to him.

"Bloodthirsty villains." She closed her eyes. Her throat was swelling. "I'm sorry, lads. I didn't mean—Da?"

But her father had turned away. "Lord, you'll find those knights laid out in the square. I left them for the crows, but they're yours if you like. Where's the miller? Arnulf, here's your lad Tig. You were saying he'd been stolen, but look, he's back."

The crowd parted, revealing the miller. He seemed much smaller than Drest remembered.

Tig rushed to his foster father and took his hand. "Father, we're safe. The knights that took me treated me well, and—it sounds as if Grimbol has saved this village again."

Arnulf stared at Tig. His shaking fingers closed around the boy's. "I did not even try to stop them when they took you. I should have tried, I—" Tears dribbled down his wrinkled cheeks. "I am not much of a father to you."

Tig drew Arnulf into an embrace. "You are the best of

all fathers, the kindest and the most thoughtful, though you worry too much. I am capable of great things, remember. I became friend to those knights, and they've come back to the village as Lord Faintree's men, and now *they'll* protect him."

"There are more knights in this village?" Grimbol hooked his thumb in his belt by his dagger. "Where?"

"They are all faithful men," said Emerick. "Grimbol, these are men I can count on. As I can count on you. Come meet them in friendship."

Grimbol glanced at each of his sons, and last at Drest.

"If that's your *order*, lord, I'll follow it," he said, his eyes still on his daughter. "*I* know how to follow orders."

Tig sprang to his feet. "If I may, Lord Faintree, I think I should let those knights know what has happened. It will take but a moment. Before they wonder and come up here on their own."

And in a flash of blue, he plunged into the crowd and out the door.

DAUGHTER AND FATHER

A day passed of work, of rebuilding the huts and tending everything that had been destroyed. Everyone labored together: Sir Reynard's castle men beside the warband, villagers with squires. Drest had walked the path all day with Tig, carrying messages and supplies, pausing to lift beams or hold up walls—or to stand with her arm around any villager who was caught by sudden tears and had to turn away. She had never seen such destruction, such suffering. And so she worked from the summer's early dawn to its late night, and slept in Elys's hut.

In the mid-morning of the second day, after finishing repairs of Wimarca's hut with Tig and Hodge, Drest wandered up to the mill. She had been with Emerick for so many days that it felt strange to have been apart. She'd missed him.

The twins and Uwen, alongside Wyneck and four men-at-arms, had done much to repair the mill, and the wheel had been built anew. Wyneck was testing the new gears, which had been smeared with pig fat and creaked as they worked.

Inside the mill's big room, Grimbol, Sir Reynard, and Emerick were sitting at the head of a long table. Drest stepped through the doorway, but paused. She was smeared with fluff, seeds, dried herbs, ash, and the sweat of hard labor.

I smell nearly as bad as sea rot.

"—and for Sir Hugh, Sir James, Sir Guy, and Sir Aimo, of all my knights, to hunt for me—" Emerick broke off. "Reynard, are you sure that *any* of my men are faithful?"

"They *will* be," Sir Reynard said, "if *you* are leading them. I'm sorry, my lord, but there are many who have fought alongside Oswyn and will take his side as long as they think he has a chance to rule. That's why we must find him quickly."

"He attacked Drest, remember, at the headland." Emerick nodded at her. "Will you come over here, lass, and tell us about that?"

She wandered up and sat in the empty space on the bench by Sir Reynard. Emerick leaned forward and smiled warmly at her.

Grimbol, at his other side, did not look at her.

"When was that?" Sir Reynard asked. "What day?"

She had to think. It seemed as if years had passed. "Five days ago."

"But he must have left at once for Harkniss, for he was

there, Oriana told Drest. Yet he'd gone before we arrived." Emerick folded his hands on the table. "God's bones, how on earth did he do that? It took us two days to reach Harkniss."

"He went by ship and then by horse," said Sir Reynard. "There's a port up the coast from the headland where we always keep a stable. You should know these things, my lord."

Emerick groaned. "So he could be *anywhere* now."

Sir Reynard patted his hand. "True, but we'll find him; your uncle likes to follow plans. It was his plan to send that group of knights to search each village—for your lifeless body, he said. Clever. They knew what they were here for: a search-and-burn. Search for someone by burning every-one out of their homes, and murder and burn the man they find. Remember those, Grimbol?"

The Mad Wolf frowned. "Aye, I remember. I served in them, and then I fled them." He rapped his knuckles against the table. "You say, Reynard, that he's following a plan. What did he mean by sending a single man to find us? That's what the villagers say, that there was one knight here alone after dark on the day I left. I've never heard of *that* done before."

"Only one knight?" Sir Reynard looked from Grimbol to Emerick. "That's against all orders."

"It was Sir Fergal," said Emerick. "He was here pretending to be a tanner from Brill's Gate. He was—hunting."

"Ah, for the wolf's head." Sir Reynard patted Drest's shoulder.

"*What's* this?" Grimbol's voice was like ice. "Who's a wolf's head?"

"You didn't know? Oswyn's marked your daughter, Grimbol. He knows how she protects Lord Faintree, and so he accuses her of his death." Sir Reynard leaned toward Drest. "But you're safe with us here, you understand."

She lowered her eyes.

The bench across from them scraped. Grimbol had risen, and was walking around the table toward the back door.

"Are we finished?" Sir Reynard asked sternly. "I think not. Grimbol, we have other matters to discuss."

"I need a word with my daughter. Drest, *come.*"

And then he was out the door.

With her throat tight, Drest slipped out from the bench and strode after him.

Grimbol was waiting in the middle of the field across from the mill.

Drest took her time on her walk toward her father's solitary figure, halting often to untangle strands of flowering purple vetch from her boots. Everything inside of her was sore—angry and hurt at once. She'd not seen her father for a full day. He'd not once come to find her and ask what she had done when they'd been apart.

Grimbol's stern face was unchanging as she approached, even when she was close. "What is this about a wolf's head? Why haven't I heard of it until now, from *that* man?" His voice was soft but brutal, a growl unlike any she had heard.

She clenched her hand over Tancored's pommel, focusing hard on the feel of that square against her skin. "I didn't want to worry you."

"Did you not think I would protect you?"

Drest fixed her narrowed eyes on her father, her lips tight.

"*Lass.*" Like a swift, sharp whip. "Do you know what it means, to be a wolf's head? It's given to the worst of men. I've never been called a wolf's head, *never,* even with all I've done. Oswyn meant for you to die. He meant for you to suffer. He meant for you to fear—"

"I know what it means!" Drest stamped on the grass. "And I know what it would have meant if I'd told you! You'd have kept me running, not stopping at villages, away from all people—"

"Aye, I'd have kept you safe! I'd have kept you on the run

with no man or woman ever seeing your face again—"

"But Da—that would be worse than what I've had! That's no life. I'd rather *die* than live like that!"

He seized her, and held her tight. "I never should have left you. I don't know what foolish notions of chivalry that lord has fed you, but Drest—ah, my lass, my lass—your life is more precious than anything. Aye, even if it *is* a life on the run."

She tried to slip away, but his hold on her was fast.

"And you think your da is a monster. I *will* be to anyone who harms my wee girl. I'll lock you up in a tower, I will, and set your brothers as guards below."

I'll climb down that tower, Drest thought. *I'll escape from any cage you try to lock me in.*

Her father's grip loosened, and Drest struggled out of it to face him on the grass.

"You're not to go anywhere without one of your brothers," Grimbol said. "Do you understand me, Drest? *Never* again. Always have a battle-mate at your side. We'll live out this threat. And I shall find Oswyn, and I shall make him look me in the eye as I take his last breath from him—aye, Drest, I *am* a monster. Now go find one of your brothers."

Grudgingly, she looked around.

"The twins. They're by the hay field. Do you see them?"

"Aye, Da." She started toward the small black figures

against the green. The itching that always came over her when she needed to run was shooting through her legs. She broke into a stride, then a jog, then a run, and then a sprint.

But instead of sprinting toward the twins, she ran for the woods.

⊹⊱ 28 ⊰⊹

DISOBEYING ORDERS

Drest heard her father's shout, but she raced on, the village at her back.

You think I'm nothing but a wee lass! I rescued you from a castle prison when you and all the lads were about to be hanged, and you still think I'm but a wee lass!

Branches tried to catch her, but she ducked through their tangle.

You told me I was to be in the war-band, but you don't treat me as if I am. Nay, I'm but your lass, weaker than any maiden I've met, and so I must be protected, and held safe—as if I don't know how to use a sword or go to battle!

She kept sprinting, and her breath became an aching dry fire in her chest.

If I wanted to be but a maiden, I'd have gone with Merewen! She tried to make me, but then she helped me, and trusted me, and knew that I could escape. Aye, a woman I barely know trusted me! Why do you trust all the lads but never me?

All at once, the woods opened up to reveal the chasm after which Phearsham Ridge had been named.

It was a furrow in the ground, separating the village and its woods from the rest of the world.

Drest's sprint rattled to a jog, then a walk. With her chest heaving, she wandered to the edge of the cliff. Tiny plants had sprouted all the way down, growing on ledges, their green leaves reaching toward the sun. Thick moss lined the lower part of the cliff. It felt like an ancient, unknown place, and she was the first to discover it.

Drest closed her eyes.

It won't ever end.

The wolf's head was a mask, a cage, a new identity. Bandit, murderer, helpless maiden.

But that's not what I am, not any of it. Drest rubbed her fist against her eyes.

Aye, I know what you are: a rot-headed squid for running into the woods by yourself. Against Da's order. Uwen's voice.

I don't want you, lad.

Aye, but you should. Did not hear Da? It's not safe for you to be alone.

I can tell if I'm safe or not. How can you? You're not real.

Nay, I'm real, you maggot-brained sparrow. I'm as real as that man who's watching you.

Drest whirled around.

A high-domed, long-jawed face in a brown hood and a brown cloak stared at her through the trees.

"Now, now," Sir Fergal said, his voice like the crackling of a fish over fire, "I've been following you for *ever* so long. You're not going to run again, are you? Let's not fight. I shan't hurt you. I need but a lock of your hair to prove I've found you, that's all. May I have one?"

He was walking slowly out from the trees as if toward a wild animal he hoped to tame. With the cliff at her back and the knight only steps away, she had no place to run.

Sir Fergal lunged, his dagger gleaming.

Drest ducked, and kicked him in the soft cushion of his stomach, but he didn't fall. He grabbed at her boot—

But not quickly enough.

She was out of his reach, on her feet, and running into the woods.

The damp leaves were as slick as stone, but Drest barely touched them in her flight. She shot between trees, her speed keeping her balance.

Sir Fergal gasped—behind her, and close. He was faster without his hauberk, and his steps were a swift echo of her own.

Twining roots swept under her feet, up a hill. The land opened to a patch of grass where trees had fallen and lay in dusty heaps. Decaying wood flew out from her steps as she scrambled over the trunks.

Sir Fergal threw himself after her, over fallen trees, through thickets of weed, reaching.

Too close.

Drest swept her dagger from its scabbard, then bolted to a stop and swung around.

He wasn't ready.

They collided and fell, a tangle of limbs.

Drest had fallen in a tangle with Uwen many times and knew how to free herself first—and to come out on top.

Within seconds, she was crouching on Sir Fergal's chest with all her weight, her knees in his stomach, her right hand on his wrist, though he'd dropped his knife, and her left holding her dagger to his throat.

"Don't move," Drest panted. Her heart beat a fierce patter. "Don't move, or I'll slay you."

He twitched against her knife. A faint red line appeared between the blade and his skin.

And then, all at once, he tensed. Taking deep, shuddering breaths through his nose, he waited, mouth tight, eyes shut, eyelids trembling.

Do it. Gobin's voice. *He's waiting for you.*

He's made you suffer. He's made you scared. Nutkin, his voice more bitter than it had ever been in life. *Do it, lass.*

⊸ 29 ⊷

THE TRAITOR'S STORY

A tiny gasp came from the knight's clenched lips. It sounded like a cry.

Are you going to slay him or sit there like a snail? said Uwen.

Nay, Drest thought. *I'll take him back to his knights.*

She let go of his hand, and crawled off his chest onto the ground, ready to pounce again if he moved.

But the traitorous knight didn't budge.

She spotted his dagger in the leaves. She grabbed it, and stuck it into Tancored's scabbard beside the sword.

"Sit up," Drest said.

Sir Fergal opened his eyes a crack. Slowly, he obeyed. He sat there, hunched and shaking.

She should have felt powerful, like a warrior or knight—but instead she was uneasy. Not afraid, but unsure. This knight, this enemy, was in her power. But that did not make her feel strong.

"Have mercy," Sir Fergal whispered. "Please."

Like the mercy he showed to you? snapped Gobin.

Drest nudged the knight's back. "Don't move."

"Please do it quickly. I know I've no right to beg a favor, but I do, and if you've any pity in your heart—"

He was shaking all over now.

Drest knelt by his cloak, which hung in a rumpled heap off his back, and with her dagger cut a thin strip from the bottom. The wool was strong and thick. She pulled the man's limp hands behind him and bound them.

Then she jerked him to his knees.

The knight began to cry.

"You don't need to do that," Drest said gruffly, trying to sound vicious. But she couldn't; his hopelessness made her think of the time she'd almost slain Emerick, and she pitied him. "I'm not going to slay you unless I must. Now get up."

He struggled to his feet, breathing hard. "Why are you sparing me? And where are you taking me?"

"To the village. And I *will* slay you if you struggle and try to attack me again, but I don't slay for revenge." *Unlike my da.* She touched the dagger to his back. "Now go."

He flinched, and began walking.

For the first few minutes, they were silent.

But soon Sir Fergal began to speak in a low, trembling voice. "I've blatantly disobeyed Lord Faintree. He doesn't even need a trial to sentence me. Do you know what I'll face? A *horrible* death, worse than any—"

He stumbled.

Drest jerked him back to his feet. "Then you shouldn't have been a traitor."

"I'm not as disloyal as they think, I—have *you* ever failed?"

Drest thought, and shook her head. "Nay."

"You're lucky. I've failed in everything since I was your age. My first battle, and I could not move, not with the noise. A man came at me on a horse. I still remember his face and how I felt: like a target. I fled. Everyone saw."

In his shuddering, broken voice, he went on to tell of other battles. He'd not always fled, but he'd always flinched, and the first time he'd slain a man—

"I fainted as I dealt my blow. Only for an instant, but when I woke, he was crushing me, that man I'd slain. He'd toppled forward upon me."

Drest had heard many battle stories from her father, but none had been like these tales of humiliation and fear.

"You shouldn't have been a knight." She hadn't meant to speak much to him, but the words came out.

Sir Fergal nodded vigorously. "I didn't know that when I was a boy. I knew it when I was in battle. I'd stand amidst the chaos and think, *What is* this? *This is not who I am.* But I'd no choice. I was born to be a warrior in my lord's army."

I was born to be a warrior, Drest thought, *but it was always right for me.*

He went on: When the old Lord Faintree died and Emerick had been choosing his war-band to capture Grimbol at his camp on the sea, Sir Fergal was not asked to go.

"I went to him anyway," said the knight. "I knelt and told him I would serve him honorably. I understood him, you see: This was his chance to prove that he was as strong as his father had been. And it was *my* chance to prove that I was more of a man than anyone knew." Sir Fergal winced. "He said no."

And when Sir Oswyn had come to him after Emerick's war-band had left, Sir Fergal had been ready to listen. Sir Oswyn had promised that under his rule, Sir Fergal the Weak would become Sir Fergal the Bold.

He used you, Drest thought. *He knew what he had to say to make you follow.*

He gave that man hope, said Wulfric's voice. *Hope in the darkness can be a powerful weapon.*

Sir Fergal cast a glance back at her. "You must think I am worse than the dirt in your fingernails. I meant you no harm. I only wanted honor. I know you won't believe that, and I can't blame you, but it's true."

They walked the rest of the way without speaking, the only sound the rustle of their steps.

At the edge of the woods, Drest paused. Before them lay

the path, and beyond it the meadow and the mill. Grimbol was in the square in the distance, Wulfric towering over him. They were talking.

"I can't go on," Sir Fergal said. "Please, I beg you. Let me free. I'll run far away, and you'll never see me again. Have mercy."

Suddenly, two dark figures seemed to materialize from the woods behind them. The twins swept up on either side.

Sir Fergal whimpered.

"Mercy would be to slay you now," said Gobin, "before *your* lord or *our* da sees you. Drest, turn your back. This will take but a moment."

Drest grabbed the wool rope with which she'd bound the failed knight's wrists. "Nay, Gobin," she said, "he's *my* captive. I shall do with him as I see fit."

Gobin gave a low laugh. "Lass. Come. Give him to us."

"You had us on quite the run," said Nutkin. "We must have our wee reward."

"You were following me?"

"Aye, Da told us to. You're not to be alone, you know." Gobin put his hands on hers and deftly slipped his fingers onto the wool rope beneath her grip. "Let go and turn aside. I promise it will be quick."

Sir Fergal's breath was coming faster.

"Nay." Drest glared at her favorite brother. "This man's been hunting me for days, and it's *my* choice. I've said that twice now, and I'll not say it again."

Gobin studied her. He exchanged a look with his twin and stepped back. "What do you mean to do with him?"

"I'll give him to his men."

Sir Fergal's chin sank to his chest.

Nutkin tapped her shoulder. "You handled him nicely, lass. The chase, the way you overpowered him. I don't remember teaching you how to do that."

"No one taught me that." She shook Sir Fergal's bound hands. "Go on. Forward."

They walked out of the woods, the twins flanking them, and onto the path. After a few minutes, villagers drifted out from their huts to watch. Grimbol and Wulfric turned. But no one advanced. No one moved as the girl and the slumping knight and the twins crossed through the field to the edge of the dirt square.

As they reached the center, Mordag swooped over them with a raucous call. She circled, not stopping, until Tig came running up the path.

"Drest?" Then he saw Sir Fergal, and his mouth closed. Wordlessly, he stretched out his arm. With a final harsh *creea*, Mordag landed on it.

The mill's front door opened.

Sir Reynard came out, followed by Emerick. The old knight's eyes widened.

"By God," he murmured. "You caught him."

Cold fury lit Emerick's face. "When you became a knight, Fergal, you vowed to serve Faintree Castle and its lord with honor. You have broken that vow. Take his sword, Drest. Give it to one of your brothers. They have served me with more honor than this man ever has."

Sir Fergal took a long, shuddering breath.

Drest pulled out the scabbard from his sword-belt. The loops parted, and the leather dropped to his feet. She held out the sword. Uwen strode up to her and grabbed it.

"You are no knight," Emerick went on, "no man. You are a traitor to Faintree Castle. Get on your knees. Sir Reynard, draw your sword."

The failed knight seemed to crumple. Onto his knees, bowing, his forehead on the dirt.

"Wait," said Drest—and thumped to her knees beside Fergal. She set her arm over the back of his neck. She wanted to hate this man, but somehow she understood his misery and fear. "Aye, he's a traitor, but your uncle tricked him and used him, see, and he never had a chance."

Fergal—no longer *Sir* Fergal—swallowed.

180

"Step aside, Drest." Sir Reynard did not lower his weapon. "He disobeyed a direct order from his lord."

I disobey orders.

She met Emerick's eyes. It was as if he had heard her thought; his face softened.

"What would you have us do, Drest?" Emerick said gently.

"You promised me mercy once. Do you remember? I want it now. For him."

Fergal tilted his head until his eyes met hers: wondering eyes, brimming with tears.

"If I give you a real chance, a *true* chance, to be honorable," she told him, "will you take it?"

Beneath her arm, he bowed his head in a nod.

"Do you promise?"

"Yes. And—I will prove it. I can help you. In what you need to do to save your life. I can help you find him."

"Find who?"

"Oswyn. I know where he's gone."

⇜ 30 ⇝

THE FINAL PLAN

Drest stood with her family and the castle men in the village square, the dishonored knight at her side. She'd called Emerick her captive before, but he had never really been one. Fergal was a true captive: a dangerous man who, if free, might well find a way to cut her throat despite his promise.

Though it seemed unlikely.

It was as if he were a wolf whose teeth and claws had been torn out.

But a wolf who had told them the story they needed to hear: Oswyn was on the headland.

"How many men does he have, Fergal?" Sir Reynard's voice was sharp. He'd been scowling as he'd sheathed his sword ten minutes ago.

"Eight knights. With thirty-two spearmen." He paused. "I was to go there in four days. He said he'd be there to collect . . . her head." To Drest: "I beg your pardon."

She shivered, but managed to get out in her old insolent

182

tone, "How would you have carried my head through the woods? Do you have a sack? I'd think it would have made a mess on your tunic."

Uwen snorted.

"I—I hadn't thought that far."

"You know the way to the headland, Fergal?" Sir Reynard's tone hadn't changed.

"Does *everyone* at your castle know the way to my headland?" growled Grimbol.

"No," said Fergal quickly, "but I was told to go to the sea, then walk north, and look for the rope ladders on the cliffs."

"Rope ladders," said Grimbol. "Listen close, lads: We'll take those ladders down, climb on our own ropes, and slay every man in the bowl of the camp. Aye, that's what we'll do."

"Perhaps you'd like to have *my* help with that?" murmured Sir Reynard.

Grimbol regarded him with a faint smile. "Aye, I'll take it." He went on: "Forty-one fighting men with Oswyn. And eighteen of us." He glared at the squires. "Can *you* fight?"

The boys shifted.

"Eighteen, then." With a sigh, Grimbol dropped to his knees on the dirt and unsheathed his dagger. "We'll have to hunt him down. Lads, are you up for a hunt at the headland?"

Drest's brothers all nodded. None of them smiled.

"Reynard, mind this. I'll draw you a map of where we're going."

He drew a series of lines.

"That's the cliff no man can climb, where they have the rope ladders." He pointed. "The ravine below. There's a river in the back. Be wary of it; it's as strong as the sea. Then up here, there's the paths. Here's the camp. The cliffs here are not safe, but my lads and lass can climb them. Then here: These cliffs empty that river out into the sea, and they're the most dangerous yet."

Grimbol rose smoothly. "Lord, will you let me order your men? I must have total command down there for this to work."

"Of course. Sir Reynard, Sir Torstein, Sir Cerdic, Sir Bren—all of you spearmen as well—you'll be under Grimbol's lead out there. Do you understand?"

The castle men nodded, including Sir Reynard.

Grimbol pointed to his sons. "Each of you take a castle man as your battle-mate. Show him the way. Gobin and Nutkin, take two of them, unless they slow you. Tig, I want you to keep watch with your crow from the top of the cliff. Squires, you're up there too. You're protecting the lord. Lord, I want you to watch, but don't come down."

"I want Drest with me."

Grimbol's chin dipped in a nod. "Aye, that's what I was thinking."

"Do you not need me on the paths?" Drest said softly. "Do *I* not know the headland as well as the lads?"

"Aye, you do, but you did not follow my order when I gave it to you just now. So nay, I don't want you down there."

Drest flinched.

"I want her up with me for a wholly different reason," said Emerick slowly. "I want her at my side because that is the only way I can be confident I shall live past this battle. Someone will see me, and they will try to slay me with an arrow, or a signal to a man who's hiding at the top. I have survived the most danger I've ever faced in my life thanks to her."

She looked at him gratefully.

"As long as she stays at the top of the cliff, I do not care the reason." Grimbol slid his dagger back into its sheath and surveyed the men around him.

"This is our final chance. If we win, we gain back Faintree Castle, and Lord Faintree will be where he belongs. Castle men, you'll fulfill the vows you swore when you agreed to fight under our lord's name, in honor, in glory." Grimbol paused. "And you, my sons, this is your chance to prove that your legends are true. Remember who you

185

are: Wulfric the Strong, Thorkill the Ready, Gobin the Sly, Nutkin the Swift, Uwen the Wild—and Drest the Clever. You are the war-band of the Mad Wolf, and no one in this world or the next could stand against our power when we are together. I have trained you to crush your enemies. There are no greater enemies than these you will be facing. They shall fall like flies against us."

Grimbol rocked back on his heels.

"One word more: Slay everyone you find but Oswyn. Save *him* for me. He's put a price on my daughter's head, and I shall have my revenge." He crouched again and swept his hand across his sketch in the dirt. "Be ready to leave as soon as we have our supplies. From what the traitor says, we've no time to lose."

Grimbol eased himself to his feet and marched toward the door of the mill.

The squires gazed nervously at the knights. Drest's brothers and the castle men stood awkwardly apart. Emerick and Tig were completely still, their eyes on the dirt where the map had been.

"You haven't enough men," Fergal said tentatively. "One more will be little, but one more could help. Let me go with you, my lord."

"No," said Emerick sharply.

"Let me prove to you that I am worthy of your trust. Let me prove that my honor—"

"You *have* no honor," snapped Emerick, "not after what you've done. Drest, I want this man bound to a post in a hut with a village guard kept round him. I know you pity him, but he's dangerous, and he'll kill you if he has the chance."

"No," said Fergal. "I will never harm *her*."

But as he looked down, the swift glance he cast upon the men in the square held such malevolence that a small voice within Drest wondered if her mercy had been the right decision.

⤛ 31 ⤜

ON THE HEADLAND'S CLIFFS

It was midday, though the sky had become a murky cloud as the war-band started off. They made a curious procession: Drest's brothers in their hunt formation, each of them with a sword from the knights they had slain; then the men-at-arms with their spear points above their heads; the knights with their chain mail clinking; and the squires, who clustered nervously at the end.

The Mad Wolf led. For the first hour, Tig strode beside him, Mordag swooping among the branches. Then the boy drifted back to where Drest and Emerick walked in the middle, between Grimbol's lads and the castle men.

"What do you think of the guard I've made you?" said Tig to Drest with a wink.

She shrugged and rolled her shoulders. Nervousness had knotted all her muscles there.

"I hope you tied your captive well, lass," Gobin called back. "I've a bad feeling, and I hope it's not him creeping after us."

She *had* tied Fergal carefully with the kinds of knots that

Thorkill had shown her long ago, knots that would take even *her* nimble fingers hours to untie. And she'd whispered to him that everything would be well when they succeeded, as they would, thanks to his help.

"But it doesn't matter." The failed knight had met her eyes in the darkness of the hut where she'd bound him. "Lord Faintree will never forgive me. If he succeeds, I will be taken to the castle and executed within days. If Oswyn wins, I shall be slaughtered where I stand. If you would only let me go—"

"I *can't* let you go. You have to understand that."

His smile had been faint. "Letting me go would be the bravest deed of all. And coming with me—think of it, lass: I'll protect you with my life, as if you were my own daughter, and we could run far from here, and be safe."

"I am not as much of a fool as *that*."

Emerick's soft voice broke her from her thoughts: "I can hardly believe this will be over soon. And also, what must happen for it to succeed." He met Drest's eyes. "I've never hated my uncle. It feels strange—wrong—to wish for his death like this. My father—he wasn't fond of Oswyn, but he never wished him dead."

"You don't have to wish it," Tig said. "Grimbol will take care of it. Just think past it to what lies ahead: You'll be home with a whole castle of faithful men."

189

"God's bones, I hope they're faithful." Emerick rubbed together his shaking hands. "I keep thinking there is something we've forgotten, something we should have done. If we don't succeed—"

"If we don't succeed, we'll still go to Faintree Castle and meet Lady de Moys," Drest said. "You'll get back your castle one way or another, Emerick."

"But that way—it would be a battle between two powerful armies. I should have spoken to her, and warned her. Oswyn will bring his whole might down upon her—"

"Nay, he doesn't know she's there; *she'll* bring *her* might down upon him. And her fury."

"Yes, that's right. I should think only of that: that we *will* succeed, somehow. But I wonder at what cost." Emerick frowned.

"Don't think of it," urged Tig. "Think of the headland, bright and open—"

"It'll be cloudy and open," interrupted Nutkin from ahead.

"—the headland, cloudy and open," Tig went on. "All the traitors will be on their knees—"

"They'll be on their backs and dead," called Gobin.

"—on their backs or knees, and Emerick, you'll stand before them with joy in your heart and know that your castle—"

"No, actually, I *won't* stand before them; I'll be up on the cliff with you and Drest."

Tig narrowed his eyes in mock anger. "Do you want to hear my tale of your victory or not? All I'm saying is that this will soon be over, and you can't think of *shoulds* and *mights* just now."

Above his head, Mordag made a rattling sound in her throat as if in agreement.

"Aye, don't drop your courage, lord," Uwen called. "You'll need it for the battle."

"He hasn't dropped his courage, you rat-faced pool of eel slime," Drest shot back. "He's doing what good lords do: thinking about all that *should* and *might* happen."

"You prickle-headed, bat-tongued—" Uwen stopped, then mumbled: "Nutkin, is that what lords are supposed to do?"

"I haven't the faintest idea."

The woods grew thicker. The wind rose, tugging at their hair and tunics. No one spoke as they strode on.

They passed the mossy fallen log where Drest, Emerick, and Tig had rested in their flight from Phearsham Ridge six days ago. Drest glanced at it longingly. If Grimbol hadn't been so far ahead, she would have asked if they could stop for Emerick to rest: He was staggering along with a permanent wince.

But also, she was afraid. A thick, dark dread had gathered in the pit of her stomach, and the weight in her chest felt like a boulder.

She was going home, yet it was not home, yet it would decide her world.

After another hour, they reached the shore.

The sea was wild. It thundered against its banks, tossing foam from its waves.

The war-band stopped. Grimbol went among the men, handing out sheepskin flasks, small meat pies that the villagers had rushed to make, and muttering a word of encouragement to each, even the squires.

"Are we close, Grimbol?" Emerick asked when the Mad Wolf came near.

"Aye, lord. Another hour or so, and then we'll be at the cliffs. We'll go deeper into the woods to follow the river. If there are men watching for us, we'll find them." He patted Drest's shoulder, a pained half-smile on his lips, but didn't speak to her.

Their rest was short, and they walked away from the sea, heading back into the deep woods.

Trees, and nothing but, surrounded Drest and the war-band. Soon she saw a burned-out pile of coals, black and old, that sparked a memory: of her journey with Emerick not so long ago.

"If I'm not mistaken," he murmured, "that's where we cooked our first hare together. And where Jupp the bandit ate it."

They exchanged wan smiles.

More trees, and a trickle of water, which became a greater stream. The war-band paused to drink.

The river grew wider, then wider, then was churning alongside their makeshift trail, the water a roar like the sea itself. Drest's ears grew numb from the noise.

Something was wrong.

The air felt heavy. The river seemed too loud.

Her brothers walked with their shoulders bent, their bodies tense and ready to fly.

Tig carried Mordag on his arm, but held her wings to keep her from warning the enemy of their approach with her calls of alarm. Her head never stopped turning, her black eyes fixing on the woods around them with an eerie, blank look.

And as they walked, Drest thought of the people she'd left behind:

Elys and Wimarca and all the others from Phearsham Ridge.

Fergal, who had betrayed both his masters: first Emerick, then Oswyn.

Lady de Moys, whom she would soon meet on the

road to Faintree Castle, the Harkniss army at her heels.

The woman in the passageway in Harkniss Castle who had been kind.

Merewen—who had risked her life to save Drest's.

Suddenly, they were at the cliff. Not far from where they stood, the river rushed against its banks and thundered down in a foaming waterfall.

"Gobin, Nutkin, go along the edge," Grimbol said. "Draw up the ladders, but for one. Drop two of our ropes."

The twins nodded, the ropes they had brought from the village in their arms, and darted off into the trees.

Grimbol waited.

Within minutes, the twins were back.

"Five rope ladders," Nutkin said. "We left the nearest one."

"Five," Grimbol mused. "I wonder why they set up five. They shouldn't have needed so many for forty-one men."

Then he walked before the war-band.

"Gobin and Nutkin, it's time for you to go. Reynard, pick two knights and two men-at-arms to follow them."

The twins sauntered up to Drest.

"Keep a good watch for us, lass," Nutkin said.

"And be ready with your sword if you need it," said Gobin.

And then they went to one of the ropes that they'd tied to a tree, and slipped over the cliff's edge and down.

Sir Reynard murmured to two of the knights, then nodded at two spearmen. The four men started down the one rope ladder, each one at another's heels.

"Thorkill and Uwen, your turn." Grimbol pointed at a knight, then two men-at-arms.

Drest's brothers approached her.

"Be brave, lass," said Thorkill, and set his hand on her cheek.

Uwen grabbed her, squeezed, then let her go.

The lads started down the rope, and the knight and two spearmen went down the ladder.

"Wulfric," said the Mad Wolf without turning around. "And the rest of you castle men but Reynard."

Drest's eldest brother held her in a long embrace, then kissed both her cheeks. As she watched him go, a lump grew in her throat.

"Reynard, go down with me now."

Sir Reynard murmured a final word to Emerick, then approached Drest. "I would ask you to have courage and take care of his lordship, but I know you will." He gave her a short bow, then started down the rope ladder with a grim face.

Grimbol watched from the brink until Sir Reynard was on the ground, then knelt and pulled up the ladder. "Drest?"

She went to his side.

"Take care of yourself first and most, my girl." He kissed her forehead. "I shall return."

And then the Mad Wolf started down the rope.

Forty-one castle men, Drest thought. *Against but eighteen— nay, seventeen without me.*

Aye, but seventeen like us? Uwen's voice in her mind laughed. *They'll be dripping from our boots when we're done with them, like the squashed snails they are.*

"Stay away from the edge, Drest," called Emerick softly. "Don't let them see you."

She nodded, and began to pull away—but a movement in the ravine caught her eye.

Men were emerging from the mist, men in chain mail, shields and swords in their hands.

They were more than forty-one.

Far more.

⤙ 32 ⤚

THE BATTLE

A trap, Drest thought. *Fergal must have known.* She opened her mouth to shout a warning.

But her father had noticed the army. He and Sir Reynard were side by side near the foot of the cliff, exchanging a word. Sir Reynard called something to his men.

Suddenly, all the loyal knights and men-at-arms swung around, weapons bristling, to face her family. The lads stood with the river at their backs, the mist that was rising from it hiding its waters.

"Nay," said Drest, her heart in her throat. "Emerick, your men are attacking my brothers."

Not attacking, though, not yet. They were closing in on them.

The Mad Wolf's war-band scattered: The twins slipped into the mist by the thundering river. Then they were gone, and Thorkill too.

The army surged bellowing from their bank of fog.

The crash of metal, more shouting—then a cry broke through.

Uwen's.

He was crouching on the ground, a hand to his bleeding shoulder. The knight who had attacked him raised his sword for the killing blow—

He crumpled, struck by Wulfric's blade.

Every form was in constant motion. Everywhere, weapons flashed.

Drest's father and brothers seemed very small among them.

Even Wulfric, who was now surrounded.

But then Thorkill was beside him, and the two loomed over Uwen. Thorkill crashed every blade that neared. Wulfric ducked one blow, and rose with his sword swinging.

The twins appeared, lunging over to help, but spearmen and knights cut them off. In seconds they shifted, standing back to back, pivoting in unison, their swords weaving to block every blow.

She could not see the loyal knights, not even Sir Reynard's dark face.

"Hie to the eagle's roost!" roared Grimbol.

Suddenly, her brothers darted, each in a different direction. Wulfric had Uwen under his arm and was running toward the river, pursued by three knights—

"Nay," Drest whispered. That water was as fierce as the sea. It would sweep them away.

There was a splash, then an unfamiliar cry. Wulfric, still carrying Uwen, was visible through the mist for an instant, and disappeared again.

"Drest!" Emerick seized her arm and pulled her back from the lip of the cliff.

A frantic need to move, to run, to fight—to do anything—rushed through Drest. She went back with him— but in seconds had slipped out of his grasp. "Tig, don't let him near the edge."

"Drest?" Alarm flashed in the boy's face. "You're not going down—"

"Your father's order—" Emerick began, but she cut him off.

"My da and my brothers are dying down there. And your knights have betrayed you. So his order's changed. My family needs me."

By the time she reached the cliff's edge again, the battle had moved up the banks toward the sea. All the knights were in pursuit of the Mad Wolf and his sons, but her family was gone.

Drest grabbed the rope her father had used and flew down. The fibers burned her hands raw, but she was soon at the bottom.

The mist was rolling in. Drest plunged into it—and into a man-at-arms who was fumbling with a crossbow.

"Who's there?" He reached out.

Drest dropped to her hands and knees, and rolled. As she did, she saw his bolts, all held by a leather strap, on the ground at his feet. She closed her fingers upon the bundle, and darted back into the fog.

"Who's there?" called the man again, panic lighting his voice.

"Lord Faintree is alive, you traitor," Drest shot back, and slipped deeper into the mist.

She knew the ravine well. She and Uwen had hunted there often: going after squirrels and hares, but also each other. She had played hiding games there all her life. And so Drest knew which trees would hold wreaths of mist and the ones that were too sparse. It had always seemed a ghostly, eerie place, but the mist would serve her now.

She slipped past clusters of knights and castle men, stealing what supplies she could. Soon she was carrying four bundles of bolts.

Drest wove her way to the river and dropped each bundle into the violent rush of water, which grabbed them from her hands. With the thundering river filling her ears, she looked around.

The mist was dense, enough to blur the woods.

Drest rose and darted between the spindly trees, taking care to step lightly.

Soon the river's roar had faded behind her, and the woods were quiet and still.

A stick crunched.

It was no more than three steps away.

Drest dropped to the ground.

A figure in chain mail showed briefly through the fog.

"Grimbol?" whispered Sir Reynard's voice. "Is that you?"

There was silence, then the muted clink of mail. He was leaning against a tree, and had put back his hood. He was running his hand over his face and hair.

"Traitor," Drest whispered.

Sir Reynard straightened, but she had already slipped away.

Where had her family gone? Had they reached the eagle's roost, the highest point of the headland? It was above the place where Emerick had fallen on the day of the invasion, and had the best defense of her home. Grimbol had taught Drest and her brothers how to position themselves around the stones and fight attackers below. There was no room for more than two men at a time on the path. And two men would be easy enough for the war-band to slay.

Not if they have crossbows, Drest thought, her stomach sinking. *Not if they stand back and have their weapons aimed and ready for you.*

She had to find her father, and warn him.

Drest followed the river, ducking between trees, her eyes constantly scanning. When she saw a knight or bowman, she would freeze and wait for him to turn his march away, and then she would rush on. Eight castle men were posted in the ravine. Some had crossbows, others spears.

At last, she was at the end of the ravine where the waterfall thundered over the sea cliffs in a foaming rage. Beside it, an uneven cliff stretched up toward the eagle's roost. That cliff was not an easy climb, and dangerous with the waterfall behind it, but Drest and Uwen had made it their duty to learn to climb that spot.

Only, she had never climbed it when Uwen wasn't there at the bottom to catch her in case she slipped. And twice she *had* slipped, sending both her and her brother perilously close to the hungry river.

Drest grabbed one of the ledges and pulled herself up. Tancored's scabbard scraped against the soil. The cliff side was slippery, damp with the waterfall's spray. Careful of each grip, she climbed, and finally reached the brink of rough reddish stone at the top. Drest hauled herself up. She was there at last, at the highest point, right near the eagle's roost.

She stood. The wind gusted around her, pushing her back against the cliff's edge. Drest shoved forward, and looked up to where her family would be waiting.

But her family wasn't there.

Sir Oswyn was sitting at the edge of the boulder, two men-at-arms beside him. Gaunt, pale, in his silver chain mail hauberk with his sword in his hand and a brutality like her father's in his pale blue eyes.

"I was wondering when I'd see you again," he said in his bitter, cruel voice. "Wolf's head."

⊰ 33 ⊱

SIR OSWYN

A wisp of rage began in her chest, and spread like fire.

"The *real* Lord Faintree's people are looking for you," Drest retorted. *"Traitor."*

She almost jerked Tancored from its scabbard.

Wait! cried Gobin's voice. *Look behind you!*

She turned—and ducked to avoid the blow that a knight at her back was swinging.

Go down the cliff again! Nutkin's voice. *Quick, lass! You're surrounded!*

She dropped on her knees and scrambled back, and disappeared over the edge.

"Climb after her!" roared Sir Oswyn.

Her boot slipped on the wet stone, but Drest found a lower hold. Then another.

A knight heaved a leg over the brink. But his foot had no purchase, and skittered at once. Half his body slid off the cliff above Drest.

She clung to her stone, pressing herself close to the dirt

and the grass. If he fell and struck her, he'd knock away her grip—

But he'd gained a hold and, grunting, pulled himself back up.

"Are you such a coward?" bellowed Sir Oswyn.

"It's too slippery, sir! And the waterfall below—"

"Get out of my way!"

Sir Oswyn's leg appeared above her, and he began to descend. Hand over hand, his chain mail creaking.

He knows how to climb, Drest thought with a chill.

It was a race down the cliff.

And she would lose unless she was faster.

But if you reach the bottom first, you'll have time to draw your sword, said Gobin's voice. *And slay him.*

Drest lifted her hand, and let herself slide.

Clumps of soil fragmented into slimy chunks between her fingers. Each foothold crumbled into pieces beneath her weight. She was rushing, tumbling, falling—

At last, her boots hit the ground. Stone pebbles and pellets of mud rattled down upon her. Drest closed her eyes, breathing hard, waiting until she felt her balance. Then she stepped back and drew Tancored with an even swish.

The sword was heavy on her arm—too heavy. Drest winced; she should have practiced with it to grow accustomed to its feel and how it swung.

Sir Oswyn thumped onto the ground. He drew his sword and lunged at once, forcing her near the roaring water.

Drest pivoted, and leaped away from the river, toward the bank she had just descended. He tried to catch her with his free hand, but his step slipped in the mud.

She could push him in the river if she rushed—

But the moment was gone.

"Whelp of the devil." Sir Oswyn was breathing hard. "The rest of my men are coming down an easier path. Give yourself up. Tell me where you've hidden my nephew."

Tancored's weight ached on her arm. "Do you not know that Grimbol's whelps never give up? It's a code of our war-band, see."

She slashed.

Sir Oswyn dodged, then lunged again.

She dodged, but the blade met her leg, tearing her hose. It was a light cut, but had enough of a sting to make her grit her teeth.

He lowered his sword, and she took the chance—swooping in at him with a rising tide, a move that would cut his shoulder or neck.

"God's blood!" roared Sir Oswyn, and threw himself aside—but as he did so, he dropped his blow, swinging hard at her feet.

Drest leaped over the blade, and caught it with Tancored

on its way up. Steel screamed against steel for a horrible, grating instant—and the swords parted.

Suddenly, Sir Oswyn's hand shot out and clamped on to her shoulder. She ripped free, but he grabbed her again, and threw her down.

Drest's elbows slammed against the dirt. She tried to scramble up, but his boot pounded upon her stomach, and stayed there, pinning her, his knee bent. Drest suppressed her moan and swung her sword in time to block his blow at her head.

But his blow was fierce. It knocked her sword from her hand.

Tancored!

The sword thumped out of her reach, over the bank to the river's edge. Its hilt teetered, the square pommel nearly touching the water.

Nay!

It was a heavy sword, a sword for a fighting man. As if it had decided that it was done fighting for *her* for good, Tancored slipped into the water, hilt-first.

"Where is my nephew?" Sir Oswyn lowered his sword, its point hovering over her chest. "I know you've kept him safe all these days. Tell me where he is, and I'll spare you."

But in that movement, his balance shifted—Drest felt it, the slight lifting of his foot. She threw herself to the side, twisting out from under him, then rolled back, back, until she was away. As she sprang to her feet, she drew her dagger.

"My *God*," Sir Oswyn gasped. "I have never seen a creature move as fast as you. What is your name, beast?"

"It's Drest, like the Picts. Remember it."

"Oh, I will."

Suddenly he was beside her, shoving her, his sword knocking away her dagger into the river at her back, where it fell with a muted plop.

Gone.

He stepped back and swung at her ribs.

Drest dove toward the muddy cliff, curling up when she hit the ground, then flew to her feet.

The ravine was before her, the trees beckoning, the cliffs with the ropes just beyond. She had an instant to start running toward the cliffs, an instant in which she might escape.

Yet another chance lay before her.

Sir Oswyn's back was to the river.

If she moved quickly, she might push him in. But it would take more than a push.

She would have to throw herself in too. She would have to be brave enough to risk everything.

Merewen risked everything.

Drest flung herself against Sir Oswyn with all her weight.

And closed her arms around his, pinning him.

The sudden push knocked him off balance.

He strained against her, but the weight of his chain mail carried them back, back, over the lip of the bank.

And then the river was around them.

← 34 →

THE RIVER

Icy cold swept over her. Drest almost opened her mouth to scream, but forced herself to focus: It wasn't over yet.

She was still clinging to Sir Oswyn, and he was thrashing to get free. She let go of him and kicked hard, meeting his chest, pushing herself up with the blow.

As if in a dance, the water and the weight of his armor dragged the old knight down—down in a silvery glimmer, his arms reaching but helpless.

In five seconds, he was out of Drest's sight.

He's gone. I've done it.

And then the river tried to pull *her* down as well.

The waves grabbed her, crushing her against a block of stone far beneath the river's surface. Drest dug her fingers beside it, into the mud of the underwater bank, and climbed. One ragged fistful of earth, then another, the water tearing at her face and limbs. Her breath fluttered in her chest like a trapped bird.

But her holds were secure.

Hand over hand, half swimming, she slowly rose. Stones and mud came off in her hands.

Her ears were pounding with her heartbeat.

She was almost there. The lip of the bank was just above her.

Her head was starting to cloud.

Drest reached up. Her hand broke free of the water.

Another hand closed on her wrist with a bruising grip.

It hauled her to the surface and up the bank's slimy mud onto the grass. Drest coughed out water until air filled her lungs and she could feel the pebbles beneath her knees.

She was still alive.

Are you sure? Pinch yourself hard to see, sniggered Uwen's voice.

Drest raised her head—and flung an arm around Emerick's dripping shoulders.

He squeezed her, murmuring her name over and over.

"What are you doing down here?" Drest choked out. "You said before you can't swim."

"No, I can't. But we saw you go under and—and not come up."

"Nay, I came up."

She cleared her throat, coughed, and tried to sit, but was shaking too much.

"I don't know what's wrong with me," she muttered.

"You nearly drowned. That you even survived—"

"I'm a water rat."

He gave a hollow laugh. "Thank God you're a water rat, or fish, or seal, or whatever form you might take beneath the waves." He held her to him, his wet cheek against her forehead. "Just breathe."

Then Tig was beside her, hugging her as well, wiping his face with his sleeve.

It was wet with tears, Drest realized, not water. She reached out for him, and soon was holding both of her greatest friends.

A strange dizziness was engulfing her, as if she were half-asleep.

"You did it, Drest." Emerick's voice, in her ear. "He's gone. I can hardly believe it, but he's gone. Lass, you've saved my life for good, and—and nearly lost your own in doing so. Please, Drest, never do that again."

"But he's gone," she murmured, "so it was worth the risk."

Mordag's call—flying near—pierced the roar of the river and the waterfall over the cliff: a blistering, incessant string of *creeas*.

"God's breath," whispered Emerick. "They're coming. Quick, Drest, Can you stand?"

Tig was under her arm, helping her as she had always helped Emerick.

But she couldn't stand. Her legs were like reeds. They folded and she fell on her knees in the mud, gasping, each breath a burden in her lungs.

"I can't move," Drest whispered frantically.

"Hold still." Emerick was lifting her, one arm under her back, the other under her legs. "Where can we run? Tig, is there a way up that cliff before us?"

It was the cliff she had just slid down, a cliff deeply marked with the furrows she and Sir Oswyn had made in their descent.

A thunder of footsteps was nearing, and with it a chorus of clinking chain mail.

Drest raised her eyes.

Faintree Castle's army was advancing up the ravine. Sir Reynard, running, was at their head.

They were shouting, though the roar of the river muted them.

"There's nowhere to go." Emerick's voice was a shadow. "Drest, I—I cannot believe it has come to this." His arms tightened around her. "I will not let you go. They will have to hack through me before they will reach you, and then—then we will fall together."

Tig grabbed his arm. "But Emerick, your uncle is dead!

We've triumphed, we've won. Tell them that. Speak to them as their lord and they'll obey. Remember what Sir Reynard said?"

A shiver passed through Emerick, but he nodded. "God's bones, I hope you're right." With a deep breath, he faced the army.

"Let me go." Drest struggled out of his arms. She had to grab hold of his tunic to keep standing, but she was on her feet as the army surged into clear sight.

Over sixty men—in chain mail and the brown tunics of men-at-arms, spears pointing, swords drawn. They were ten paces away when Sir Reynard raised his hand and they stopped.

Suddenly, Grimbol was there, pushing through, and halted at Sir Reynard's side. The old knight grabbed Grimbol's arm—but as if to support him, not hold him back.

As if Sir Reynard were again on Emerick's side. As if he'd never left.

"She's alive?" Grimbol said, his voice a whisper against the crash of the waterfall at Emerick's back, though his lips showed his words. "My lass is alive?"

Drest leaned against Emerick. Her head was swimming. "Aye, Da, I'm alive. I don't die that easily."

Emerick's arm encircled her.

"Speak to your army," Tig urged. "Quick!"

214

The young lord took a deep breath. "Men of Faintree Castle! You stand before me, thinking I was dead, but—but I live, and—" His voice faded. "—yes, I live."

Tig raised his chin, and strode in front of Emerick. He planted himself solidly before the army.

"Lord Emerick Faintree lives!" he shouted, his voice a cry through the thundering water. "Behold your one and only lord, your *true* lord, the man who will take Faintree Castle into a new age of glory!" He paused. "And behold who stands with him. Not a vicious beast, but a legend of courage and faith. She is the warrior maiden who has saved our lord from death, and who has drawn the traitor into the waters beyond. Yes, Oswyn Faintree, with his rotting core of evil, is dead. He has gone forever, into *that*." He pointed at the pounding river behind him.

No one moved.

Tig took a step closer to the army, and though his azure tunic and black hose were muddy and torn, he could not have looked more regal. He flung out one arm in a gesture to encompass all the men. "Let the loyal among you kneel, and let the traitors stay standing."

Tig spun around and, as if he were a royal page, knelt on one knee in the mud before Emerick, head bowed.

Silence.

Emerick tensed.

Drest's fingers crept down to her sword-belt and closed over the top of the empty scabbard.

Suddenly, Grimbol and Sir Reynard fell to their knees at the river's bank, heads bowed, hands on their hearts.

And with a rattle of chain mail that sounded like a rockslide, the army did the same behind them.

Drest scanned the crowd of bowed heads—knights, spearmen, and her brothers too.

The whole army.

Not a man had remained standing.

-+- 35 -+-

THE RETURN

D rest picked at the dried mud caked on her wrist. She could barely see it in the dark, even with the flickering torches all over the deck. The wind gusted, and the ship's enormous sail strained over her head. Her legs were still wobbly, but, clinging to the side of the hull, Drest hauled herself to her feet and looked over into the black water.

Spray splashed up from where the ship's hull met the waves, spattering her face. She was abruptly cold, her legs shaking like the gorse on the headland's cliffs.

"You've lost your blanket!"

Tig came up behind her and flung the blanket over her shoulders.

"I—I need to sit," Drest muttered.

"Take my hand. I'll help you."

"Nay, lad, I'll more likely tear you off your feet." She sank to her knees, thumping painfully against the wood. "I'm all unsteady. I feel like a gull that's been swept in the waves and half drowned."

"You *are* that gull. You *have* been half drowned." Tig sat beside her and grabbed her hand. "I still can't believe you're here. I saw you go under the river—no, that's not the worst—I saw you fighting. Each time Sir Oswyn raised his sword, I thought—" He broke off, his lips trembling.

"That was just battle, Tig. It's what I've been trained to do all my life." And yet—it had been more than just battle.

She'd fought Sir Oswyn. A soldier as strong as her father. A warrior with no weakness, no mercy.

I wouldn't have slain him if I hadn't gone in with him. He might have slain me.

Drest shuddered.

Tig's arm closed around her. "You're here," he murmured. "You're here and safe. Oswyn's gone forever now. You'll never have to fight him again."

Drest squeezed his hand weakly.

"I've never seen you in a deadly fight. And that river, and that fog, and the sound of that water—" The boy's laugh was broken. "I beg your pardon, Drest, but I don't much like your home."

"Nay," she murmured, "it's not my home now."

Across the ship, Wulfric was carrying Uwen. The boy's wounded shoulder was bound with a cloth that glowed in the torchlight. Wulfric's step was sure on the rolling deck, as if he'd walked on such an unsteady surface all his life.

"He wants to see his wee sister." Wulfric knelt and gently set Uwen on the deck beside Drest. "How are you, lass?"

"I'm alive, am I not?" She nudged Uwen, whose eyes were open only a crack and whose face was ghastly pale. "What about you?"

A ragged laugh came from his throat. "I'm a gull-faced rat's bottom if I'm not."

"Well, you're a rat's bottom, so does that mean you're only half-alive?" She leaned against him. He smelled of sweat and blood.

"I—I don't know how long I'll last." Uwen's voice was a shadow of what it had just been. "It doesn't hurt anymore. I know that's bad."

Drest's stomach was hollow. "That only means that you've lost enough blood to have a fuzzy head. Nay, lad, you'll last. It's but a short ride by ship—half a day, Emerick once said—and then when we're at the castle, they'll have healers."

Tig dug in his tunic. "If it's not wet—oh, good. Wimarca gave me this for Emerick, but I think you might need it more, Uwen." He withdrew a handful of herbs.

"What do I do with them?" said the boy in a slurred voice.

"Eat them," said Drest. "Open your mouth, lad." She grabbed a pellet of stems and seeds and set it against her brother's tongue.

He chewed, and then stopped and was quiet—too quiet, Drest thought with alarm. She started to rise.

"No, don't move," said Tig softly. "They've made him fall asleep. That's good."

"Aye, lass, let him rest." Wulfric stood and set his hand on the railing, looking out at the sea.

Drest nestled against Uwen, the battle-mate of all her youth, and closed her eyes.

Above her, the sail thumped with a new gust of wind.

"How is she, lad?" It was Wulfric, quiet.

"I don't know for sure." Tig, just as quiet. "She sounds like herself. *I* feel as if I'm going to start weeping at any moment, however."

"You and our da. For him to see her go under the river like that—" Wulfric sighed. "I was with the twins. They wanted to rush in and help her, but it wasn't safe. She was fighting well, but if she'd been distracted, he would have had her. I held them back. But if that had been the wrong choice—" His voice broke. "Ah, lad, I feel like weeping too."

Drest wanted to open her eyes, but they were heavy.

"Is she resting?" Now it was Thorkill's voice.

"Aye, lad. With her battle-mate. Remember when we were like that?"

Thorkill gave a soft laugh. "Aye, after our first battle. I could barely stand. And that quiet—"

"The quiet that comes when all is still." Wulfric's voice, faded. "It's never been that quiet since."

"Why is that?" Tig asked. "You've been to many battles, haven't you? And all those battles end."

"Aye, but there's always another," said Thorkill. "And after your second, you realize that there will be another, and another. They're never truly done."

Boards creaked, and someone warm settled on the deck beside Drest.

Another warm someone joined him.

"I don't like ships." Gobin's voice, muted. "How's my wee Drest?"

"There's no color in her face." Nutkin's voice.

"She's resting." Thorkill. "She's worked hard, our brave lass."

Nutkin gave a faint laugh. "She called herself a legend once. After watching what she did today, I'd say she's right."

Gobin shuddered. "But it tears some years off of a lad's life, doesn't it, to see his wee sister battling a man who wants nothing more than to cut her in two."

"Hush," murmured Wulfric. "Don't speak of that near her."

A pause, so long that Drest almost fell asleep. But then Wulfric resumed his low murmur: "When she wakes, all will be different. She'll know that life has changed, and she'll never again be the wee lass we've known. That fog—you all know what I mean—she'll start feeling that soon. Keep a close eye on her, and help her. But do it as you would for one of us, not our wee Drest, for she'll never be that again."

← 36 →

THE WAR-BAND DECIDES

When Drest opened her eyes, it was still dark, and she was lying on the deck on a pile of blankets. Tig was her only companion.

"Where's my family?" She sat up, groggy. "Are we at the castle yet?"

"We're nearly there, so your father is talking about what to do. With Emerick." Tig rose and held out his hand. "If you can, you should join them."

She needed help to rise. But once she did, she felt stronger, and was able to stride stiffly across the deck, Tig supporting her, to where Emerick and her family were gathered.

They were on the other side of the ship, and alone: All the castle men were clustered in other spots. Sir Reynard was standing near but not with them. He flashed Drest a smile as she passed.

"I tell you, lord," Grimbol was saying as she drew close, "it will not do for us to join your men. I'm past the age where I'd have the patience to be part of another man's army. It's good of you to say that you'd take me back after all these years, but I don't want it. And your men would not like to have my lads and me among them."

"But Grimbol, can you not see what I now have?" Emerick leaned close to her father. "Power as I've never had before. With Oswyn dead, they have no choice but to obey me." He rocked back on his heels. "I've spoken to Reynard, and he agrees that this would be best: to honor every one of you for your bravery, and hold trial for Oswyn's most faithful men."

"Hold trial if you wish, but we'll not be your soldiers." The Mad Wolf grimaced. "I cannot live under another man's yoke. And my lads cannot either."

"But you'd be under no yoke," Emerick insisted. "A castle needs men who will come and go as they please—"

"My lads will fight only for *me,* not *you.* There, I've said it. We're loyal, but not as loyal as you'd need us to be."

Emerick glanced around at the war-band. "Is that true? Would none of you accept the bonds that come with full loyalty to my castle?"

Each of Drest's brothers looked at their father.

"I'm sorry, lord," Grimbol said, "but having freedom— it's how we've always lived. It would be hard to change."

Emerick's gaze lowered, but flicked to Drest before it did.

"You didn't ask me," she said.

Nutkin and Uwen made room for her between them,

and, with Tig still beneath her arm, Drest slipped into her place. Uwen, who was leaning on Thorkill, grinned at her.

"Have we both turned feeble?" he scoffed.

"*You're* wounded badly, and *she's* half-drowned having just saved all of us," growled Gobin, "so shut it."

Drest wrinkled her nose at Uwen, then looked up at Emerick. "I don't need my freedom the way the lads do. I can find it at the castle. So aye, you can tell Sir Reynard that I'll gladly live there as your guard."

Emerick's eyes sparkled and his smile was broad. "You'll let me fulfill my promise to you at last: of a proper bed, fine clothes, as many meals as you wish to eat each day. And I'll add to it a new weapon that will suit you like a glove."

"And your friendship," Drest said. "Forever. That's the only part I really want."

He ducked past her brothers, pushing his way to her side, and embraced her, almost as tightly as he had when he had pulled her from the headland's river.

Silence, but for the waves slapping against the ship's hull.

Emerick looked back at Drest's brothers. "What do the rest of you say? Will you not be like your sister and stand as warriors at my castle? I will give you not only your freedom but roles over other men, for I have no one who is as fine a warrior as any one of you. I can see Gobin the Sly and Nutkin the Swift training a scouting party to move in silence in the woods. I can see Wulfric the Strong helping my knights build their own strength to be more like his. I can see Thorkill the Ready with a fleet of bowman at his heels, commanding their ranks. And Uwen the Wild— I can see him teaching our squires that a lad of their age need not flinch when a man like your father asks if they can fight."

"Don't try to tempt them." Grimbol's voice was harsh. "How can you be sure your men will not stab my lads in the back the first chance they get?"

"Because I would punish any traitor who tried to harm them with the most brutal death I know. Your sons would be my special guard, and you, Grimbol—you would be not only their leader but my advisor."

The old warrior snorted. "Do you think I'm a fool, lord? That's weak flattery."

Emerick raised his chin. "You're a battle-hardened soldier who has outsmarted my father's men for most of my life. I need you. To tell me how to make my men powerful, but also how to keep them loyal. And how to be a good lord. I want to be better than my father, to not fail the way he failed, but I cannot do that alone. I don't know how."

Silence. The sea air gusted against the sail.

Emerick looked around at the lads again. "Have any of you changed your minds?"

Grimbol cleared his throat. "Uwen? What do you say?"

"Have I a choice, Da?" Uwen hesitated. "If I do, I want to live at the castle."

The old warrior grunted. "Gobin and Nutkin?"

The twins looked at each other.

"I don't think it would be right for us to leave Drest," said Gobin slowly.

"Aye, and we'll need to teach her how to climb *your* cliffs, lord," added Nutkin.

Drest met their eyes. The twins winked.

Grimbol pivoted to face his second-eldest son. "Thorkill? What do you say?"

The young warrior stroked his curly ginger beard. "I can see myself leading a band of castle men. Nay, they do not disgust me as they do you, Da."

The old warrior faced his eldest son. "What of you?"

Wulfric looked pensive. "If I can be useful there, I'll do it."

With a sigh Grimbol turned back to Emerick. "I cannot leave my lads. If you meant what you say, I'll go with you as well."

Emerick bowed. "Thank you. Thank you all. Now let me give this happy news to Reynard."

"I'm not sure he'd call it *happy*," Grimbol muttered as Emerick stepped away.

"Funny, how all this has turned out," Gobin said. "Lord

Faintree said he'd rather die than serve in our war-band. And now look at *us* about to serve in *his*."

Thorkill let out a booming laugh. "I'm sorry, Da, but to lead a group of men—*and* when he spoke of food, of as many meals as we wanted each day—"

"The *bed!*" cried Uwen. "Did you not hear what he said about that? I shall sleep for days upon a *bed*, a real *bed!*"

"What was that about new clothes? I think black silk tunics would do well for us." Gobin nudged his twin. "With black cloaks."

"Aye, we'll look like the most sinister phantoms these knights could imagine."

The twins burst out laughing.

"I do not mean to speak lightly of this, Da," said Wulfric, "but I *could* use a proper sword. These swords I've had of late do not fit my arm."

"I'd like a proper tunic." Thorkill fingered the torn fabric on his chest. "With cords of silken thread."

"Pots of cream and papers of cheese," giggled Nutkin.

"We'll float in the kitchen and steal them, then float out, and leave everyone a-tremble!" Gobin leaned into his brother, his hand over his mouth.

"*Beds!*" cried Uwen. "What about you, Drest? Are *you* longing for a real bed?"

But Drest was not smiling. All her brothers' mirth had

warmed her, but her father's words came back to haunt her mind: What if any knight was jealous of the honors given her family?

"Will we be safe?" she asked softly.

Instantly, her brothers' smiles disappeared.

Grimbol reached out to his daughter, setting his hand upon her cheek. "You are right to worry. But the lord is right as well: He has power that he'd never had, now with Oswyn gone. And with me at his side, they'll know it will be not safe to defy him."

The old warrior looked among his sons.

"Lads," he went on, "go wander the deck. You're castle men now, and you may as well get used to walking among the rest." He went to Drest's side and slipped his arm around her waist, holding her up. "I've got her, Tig. You go on too. Let her old father hold her this once."

Reluctantly, the lads parted, Tig drifting away last of all, leaving Drest and Grimbol alone.

"Can we sit, Da?" Drest asked. "My legs are going all wobbly on me again. Something's wrong with me. I hope it's just the ship."

"Ah, lass, there's naught that's wrong with you. It comes from battle for every one of us."

He led her to the railing and helped her down, then sat beside her.

Drest leaned against her father, breathing in the cold sea air.

"You've done well, my lass," Grimbol said. "I wanted to tell you that. I saw only the end of your battle, and how you ducked and twisted like a snake. You're better at that than even the twins." His eyes glittered. "But I had no time to save you."

"You didn't need to, Da. I don't always need you to save me."

He gave a hollow laugh. "You sound like your mother. She told me those very words a long time ago. That was when I knew I loved her more than any woman on earth."

Drest raised her head. "My *mother*? You've never mentioned my mother before."

"Have I not?" He was quiet. "Nay, I've not because I did not want you to regret."

"Regret what? Da, who was she?"

His face was troubled. "Perhaps you are strong enough to hear her tale, but it is not one that will soothe you." He closed his eyes and sighed. "Your mother, lass, was a healer who once saved my life. Her name was Merewen."

⤛ 37 ⤜

GRIMBOL'S TALE

Drest didn't move. Everything within her had turned cold.

"I don't know if she's still alive now," Grimbol went on slowly. "She would not let any man mark her fate, and men don't take that kindly."

Drest opened her mouth, then closed it.

Merewen.

She'd known Grimbol, she'd once said.

She'd wanted to take Drest far away, to a village where they would live together.

She'd been willing to give her life for Drest by the castle wall.

But she had never told the truth, though she'd had the chance. As if she did not want her daughter to know.

Drest kept silent.

"She was the one who healed me," Grimbol was saying, "so I could go to the old Lord Faintree and be told that I had fallen from his grace. Aye, lass, it was *that* battle, the one that decided everything. She followed me on my walk to the castle. She saw the old lord cast me away. She took me to Launceford, to her hut. I healed on her bed, and there planned my revenge. I made my first war-band in her town."

For a moment, Drest heard only the pounding of her heart.

"When my Lady Celestria died, I feared the castle. They'd blame me, I knew, and seek not just me in revenge but my wee lads as well. So I fetched your brothers from their villages, and their mothers gave me them gladly, for they knew they'd all perish if my lads stayed. The headland was my secret, and that's where I went. With the lads. And Merewen. And you." He glanced at his daughter. "I will tell you this, lass, though it shames me: Your mother did not come willingly."

Drest winced.

Had she been like me and did not want a life of hiding?

"Why was she not there when I was growing up?" Drest asked softly.

"Because she left when you had seen but one year." Grimbol frowned. "She wanted to take you. I did not let her. Aye, it might have been safe by then, but I would not see you grow up a lass like any other in a village. I wanted you to grow up with the lads, to be as strong as they. I wanted you to be able to hold your own against any man, be he villager or soldier. Or knight."

Because of Celestria, Drest realized with a start. *You'd seen her die by a knight's blow. You wanted to be sure that your own wee lass would never fall like that.*

"Your mother spoke fierce words to me, but in the end, she agreed. And so we parted forever."

Grimbol squeezed his daughter's hand and let it go.

"Would you have rather grown up in a town with a mother? I've never thought to ask you. It would have been a quiet life, and you've not had that. But I always thought you'd have a better life with us." He faltered. "Was I wrong?"

That was what Merewen had been talking about: a quiet life in a hut like Elys's.

And in a village—fetching water, frying hearth bread, picking herbs. Having time to rest in the sun. Knowing other lasses. Spending every night inside.

Yet—if she'd grown up that way, it would have been a life knowing nothing else—not what it felt like to carry a sword, or climb a cliff, or run until her breath had shriveled up in her chest.

A quiet, safe life as someone else.

She met her father's eyes. He was cringing, waiting for her answer.

233

"Da," Drest said softly, "that's a foolish question. Did you not see me fighting out there? Do you not know what I am?" She set her hand on his. "I'm a warrior. I've always known that."

He drew his daughter to him and held her tightly in his arms. "A true warrior, and the best one of my war-band. Braver and stronger than the rest. Lass, I could not be prouder of you."

But she pulled away. "Da, the lads are your war-band. Not me. I'm sorry, but I can't follow your orders. I never have."

Grimbol bit his lip. But he did not say a word.

In silence they sat together, the waves thrashing against the wooden hull at Drest's side. Shadows drifted over the deck between the torchlight like islands. Drest watched them combine and shift.

Sir Reynard approached and knelt beside them. "We're nearly there. Grimbol, I must have a word with you of how we'll manage things at the castle. The lord and I were talking. For weeks, I expect, you and I must keep frequent company."

Grimbol sighed and rose. "I hope you can stand it, Reynard."

A small sigh seemed to fill Sir Reynard's chest, but he

didn't let it out. "And you, Drest—once we arrive, just stay at Lord Faintree's side, and you'll be safe."

Because of the wolf's head. She watched Grimbol and Sir Reynard wander away across the deck.

Then Emerick was beside her, beaming so much that she could not help but smile in return.

"Drest," he said, taking her hands, "we're almost home."

⤙ 38 ⤚

WOLF'S HEAD NO MORE

Lord Emerick Faintree stood at the head of the cavernous Great Hall, Sir Reynard on his left, Drest on his right. The Faintree emblem was everywhere around them—on weavings, painted in blue, and carved in stone upon the lime-washed walls.

Emerick had said that this ceremony would remove the wolf's head from Drest once and forever.

But Merewen's warning at Harkniss was vivid in her mind. Beyond the castle, those who had not heard of the ceremony would not know that the wolf's head was gone. They would not know why it had existed, just that she was marked by it. And that would be her legend.

Yet Emerick had done all he could to make this a memorable occasion.

Outside on the bailey, long trestle tables had been set up, piled high with food—roasted game birds, thick breads, fish pies, and berry custards—all set out to feed the masses of villagers who were crowding in the back of the Great

Hall behind the knights and the castle folk. Arnulf, Idony, and Wyneck had come, as well as Elys and Torold and others from Phearsham Ridge; and many more from other villages too, far more, even, than had come to watch Grimbol and his war-band hang over a fortnight ago. It wasn't a mob: It was nearly a whole town packed into that room and on the grass beyond the doors.

Inside, color filled the floor of the Great Hall. All the knights and men-at-arms were dressed in finery. The Mad Wolf and his sons were clothed like them: in tunics of bright green, blue, or red, the fabric adorned with silken cords—except the twins, who wore the black silk they had wanted and looked like phantoms in the crowd.

Emerick was resplendent in an azure tunic with a gold-threaded black mantle on his shoulders. A sword with a gleaming hilt hung at his hip.

Drest, by his side, wore the plainest garb: a long tunic of thin, blindingly white wool, with only a single leather belt. Tig had told her that the color meant rebirth and a new life.

She wanted to believe it could happen.

So much *had* happened in the days since they had returned to Faintree Castle.

She had spent four nights in a bed near the window of Emerick's chamber, a bed stuffed with straw, unbelievably soft, in a wooden frame. She had sat at his side at trestle tables in the Great Hall and eaten the strangest foods: fried eels in a cream sauce with honey, pike roasted whole with blackened new apples, and sharply seasoned soups as thin as water. She'd walked the castle battlements with Tig and Sir Reynard, the sea wind whipping against her face and Mordag swooping on the current.

And she'd spent hours with Lady de Moys. The lady had been waiting on the road to Faintree Castle with her army as she had promised: reminding everyone that the young Lord Faintree had a powerful ally who would do much on his behalf. Lady de Moys had taken Drest all over the castle to meet the castle ladies, the wives and daughters of the men who lived there, and to see the way they lived: a world of weaving and healing. And stories.

All the castle ladies were there throughout the Great Hall, looking up at Emerick. Lady de Moys, in a gown the color of violets, was with her men, standing to the side, watching with cool dignity.

Tig stood with Drest's family, arms crossed, in a fresh azure tunic and black hose. His gaze had not left Drest since she had walked to the head of the hall.

They're here for me, Drest told herself.

Emerick stepped forward.

The low murmur that had filled the Great Hall abruptly silenced.

"This is a day of celebration," he called out, "a day of glory, when the world will know what has transpired during the past fortnight and how it has changed this castle forever."

Emerick surveyed the room, then turned to Drest. His eyes were unusually bright.

"Please kneel."

She flinched but obeyed. She had never knelt for him, but of course she would have to. Yet still her face burned as she stared at his fine leather boot.

In a softer voice that still echoed throughout the hall: "Please look at me."

Flushing more, she looked up.

Sir Reynard had come to his side and was holding out on the flat of his hands a dark leather scabbard. With a sword.

Am I to be punished? She glanced out at the crowd, trying to find Grimbol's face, but saw only the sea of colors.

With a quiet swish, Emerick drew the sword, then turned back to Drest and spoke in his booming castle voice: "In honor of your service to Faintree Castle, for the protection you have provided its lord at the risk of your own life—"

His voice for an instant grew hoarse.

"—for your courage in battle, for your brave acts of chivalry—"

He paused, and swallowed.

"—for your faith, for your goodness, and for your unending loyalty—for these I knight you, Drest, under the eye of God."

With great care, Emerick touched the flat of the sword to Drest's shoulders.

She barely felt it.

"Rise now in service to God as Lady Drest Madwulf— Lady Drest the *Brave*—of Faintree Castle."

She could not move. She barely felt her legs.

You cannot knight a lass.

Yet he had.

Emerick passed the sword to Sir Reynard and reached down for her hands. He drew her to her feet and turned to face the hall.

A shock had seemed to run through the crowd. No one spoke. All the faces staring up at her were openmouthed, or pinched, or stern.

Emerick's eyes hardened.

"Know the name of Lady Drest Madwulf." His voice rang out. "Know her as my bravest and most loyal knight, and my greatest friend. Do *not* forget it. Ladies, knights, soldiers, and villagers—let the news of this spread wide. Let the world know who has joined the ranks of the finest knights in the land."

Some of the Faintree men were looking at each other, their faces wide with disbelief.

Some of them were whispering.

His knights aren't going to like this, murmured Gobin's voice. *It's a good thing we're here to protect you, lass.*

The crowd shuffled.

A pair of hands began to clap, powerful hands: those of Lady de Moys. Within seconds, her guards and knights all started clapping.

It spread: Sir Reynard, Grimbol and his sons, the ladies of the castle, and last the Faintree knights, until the hall was thundering with sound.

The noise threw itself against Drest, buffeting her, drowning her. She stood with Emerick's hands on hers, her legs shaking.

He leaned down to her ear. "I beg your pardon for not warning you what I was going to do. I didn't think you would mind."

"Nay, I don't mind, but Emerick—your knights aren't going to be happy."

"They shall have to accept it." He hesitated. "And I think they will, especially if they catch a glimpse of Oriana and remember what she and her men will do if they challenge me."

Drest bit her lip. "I'm grateful, but—could you not just have removed the wolf's head?"

"Why do that when I can change your legend forever? Drest, this will be the new rumor: of how a foolish young lord has turned his friend into a maiden knight. It's unreal, improbable, fantastic—and you shall be known as the maiden knight for the rest of your life." He squeezed her hand. "Now, everyone who's knighted gets a sword. If you'll pardon me."

He let her go and took the scabbard from Sir Reynard, who handed him a sword-belt as well. Emerick knelt before Drest and buckled it around her hips, then slipped the scabbard into the loops. And last the sword.

The blade slid against the leather, its weight familiar, and right.

Emerick rose and took her hand again, and, staring defiantly out at the applauding crowd, raised her hand to his heart.

You know what he's done, don't you? Gobin's voice. *Remember that talk you had about taking risks for each other? He's just saved your life by taking a massive risk for himself. And only time will tell how this will turn out.*

242

Drest looked at the crowd, some of it hostile, but most approving, and felt as she had almost three weeks ago, standing on the headland's boulders with Borawyn on her hip, ready to venture for the first time into an unknown world: proud, and unsure, but unflinching.

Only this time, she was not alone.

epilogue

At the top of the tower, the wind whipped, but Drest stood firm against the gusts. With her sword in her hand, she skittered back across the stones, and dropped into a fighting pose.

That sword—its weight, its balance, its grace—was unlike any weapon she had carried. It felt like part of her arm.

The blade swept through the air like a fish through water—weaving, twisting, flowing—as Drest ran through her favorite moves. A circle lift, an up-and-over, a rising sun. Again and again in rapid succession, pivoting as she did so, the scabbard thumping against her leg.

Drest stopped, breathing hard. She slid her sword into its scabbard, and sighed at the familiar, comforting weight.

"Does it suit you?" said Emerick.

Drest grinned. She'd found it easier to grin of late.

"*I* think it does. You really look like yourself now. Especially with your fine azure tunic." Tig rested an arm on a merlon, his own new azure tunic bright against the cloudy sky. Mordag landed in the crenel beside him and let out a soft *caa*.

"Aye, Morvidwyn suits me well. Did you see how it moved? I've never held such a beautiful sword."

Morvidwyn—her own name for her sword—*was* beautiful: Tiny wave-like patterns covered the entire steel blade. A single blue jewel marked the pommel, which was round and one piece with the rest, the gem stamped in tight.

Drest strode across the even stones to the corner of the tower that looked out over the road. Emerick joined her, and Tig, and the three stood together, watching.

Lady de Moys and her army were leaving. Emerick had wished her farewell in the Great Hall with all his men, then led Drest and Tig to the highest point of the castle to watch the procession.

The army had passed the gatehouses and was nearing the end of the long earthen road.

"Did she ever tell you the story, Drest, of the new legend of Harkniss Castle?" Emerick asked.

"Do you mean *my* legend at Harkniss?"

"No, Lady Madwulf, your legend isn't the only one at Harkniss Castle"

Drest fixed a scowl on her face to keep back her grin. "Do you think I care about any legend but my own?"

"Do you think my knights are allowed to speak to me like that?"

"Aye, if you'll be a puffed-up, maggot-headed crab about it."

"It's better than being a—a wasp-headed boar's stomach."

Drest let out her grin. "That was a good one."

"Thank you." He reached out and took her hands. "Shall I tell you about Harkniss Castle's legend now?"

Drest settled back on her heels. "Is it a good story?"

Emerick leaned against a merlon, still holding her hands. "It's the legend of a mysterious creature who appeared on the bailey the day of our escape." He paused. "This one looked like a woman in gray, with long gray hair, a gray face, and gray eyes. She was the one who spooked the sheep, they say."

Drest held very still, her mirth gone. "Merewen," she whispered. *My mother.*

"They saw her running along the wall to the postern gate. No one dared draw near. But one guard, with the gate at his back, stayed in her path. They say that when she approached, he collapsed. They found him pale and lifeless on the ground. But after they'd rubbed his face and arms, he woke, and could speak. The creature, however, was gone. She'd disappeared."

"Did she climb the wall?"

Emerick shook his head. "No one knows. They searched but never found her."

"She escaped, then. She—she didn't die."

"Yes, this means that Merewen escaped."

Drest swallowed, her eyes suddenly wet.

Emerick's voice became soft. "Drest, I beg your pardon. I wasn't trying to upset you. I thought you'd like to know."

"Nay, I'm glad you told me. I only—I—I was worried about her." The words *She's my mother* came to her lips, but faded. That was not something she was ready to share yet. It was Merewen's secret.

And now hers as well.

"I'm glad to hear she's safe," said Tig. "I wonder if she'll come to the castle to visit once she hears the rumors of what Drest has become."

"If she does," said Emerick, "I shall welcome her with the honor she deserves. She risked her life for us, and she will be rewarded handsomely."

"Nay," said Drest slowly, "she won't come. She's not one for rewards. She may see us one day, but only if she wants to."

I wonder what she'll think when she hears what I've become,

Drest thought. *I wonder what she'd think if I told her I know the truth.*

Tig touched her shoulder. "I've thought of another poem. May I say it to you tonight?"

She nodded shyly, not looking at him. He'd been composing legend poems about her almost every day, and Emerick had been recording them with a quill on parchment. Sometimes the poems made her flush, but still she listened, sitting beside Tig in the solar on the cushioned bench that was now by the window where Sir Maldred had fallen to his death.

"I'll be happy to record it," Emerick said, "unless you want the practice, Tig."

"You shouldn't let me practice on parchment," Tig said. "Or at all. I am not learning my letters as quickly as I thought I would."

"Give it time," Emerick said gently. "And let me know if anyone bothers you about that again."

Drest and Tig exchanged glances. One squire had been seen imitating Tig's clumsy attempts to write his first letters, and the whole castle had heard. Emerick had spoken sternly to the young man. Later that afternoon, Gobin and Nutkin had gathered all the squires for a short and strangely quiet conversation. That evening in the Great

Hall, the squire who had mocked Tig had humbly apologized to him. There had been no mockery since.

It's good to have my brothers in this castle, Drest thought.

Emerick walked back across the tower and pointed at the road. "Look, the Harkniss army is gone at last. God's bones, it took long enough for her to leave. I'm grateful to her—she did everything we asked—but Oriana—" He winced. "It's not easy to have a guest in one's castle who behaves as if she owns it."

"She took Fergal," Drest said. "You owe her one for that."

Two days ago, Sir Reynard had persuaded Emerick that Fergal should suffer the punishment he was due. And for the first time, Emerick had not listened to Drest.

It was a gruesome sentence: hanging, drawing, and quartering. When she learned what that meant, Drest had begged for his life. She understood more than ever how the failed knight had been forced into a life that had been wrong for him. If she had gone with her mother as a bairn in arms and grown up as a lass in a village, she was fairly certain that she would have lashed out with her warrior blood. She understood Fergal too well.

But Emerick had refused, and so Drest had gone to Lady de Moys the day before she was to leave and begged the lady to take Fergal as a castle man, a servant, a laborer for her fields, anything that would keep him alive.

"Is that your wish?" Lady de Moys's voice had been strangely gentle. "It is customary for one who has performed heroic actions to receive a favor in thanks. You came to me when everyone else was afraid. I will give you this."

And so the lady had taken the failed knight, bound at his wrists, riding a horse led by one of her men. He would be a laborer with a guard always watching over him.

"I know you don't believe me," Fergal told Drest as he was about to be led away, "but I swear I didn't betray you. I sent you where you needed to go, and you did what I expected. But this—I did not expect this. I will never forget you, lass."

"I shall give Oriana all glory due to her. I shall never speak an evil word of her again." Emerick was starting toward the trapdoor that led to the stairs down. "And now, I must go. I have a task I might as well face. Your father, Drest, wants to tell me something about his villages. Something *else* that he did for which I must make reparation in order to win their loyalty. I wish he hadn't been so vengeful against *my* father. It's getting expensive."

Drest touched Emerick's arm. "Will you come with me instead? Tig, you too. There's something I've been wanting to show you, Emerick, and I don't want to wait any longer."

Emerick's face softened. "Of course I'll come with you."

She took his hand and led him down the stairs, past the solar with its painted lime-washed walls and tapestries, past the ornate room beside it where her father and brothers slept, then Sir Reynard's and the chambers of the other knights and servants, then lower and lower, past the Great Hall, and finally out through the iron-studded door onto the green.

Drest glanced back. The keep loomed behind her, tall and bold, its high windows open. It was the palest stone and gleamed almost like metal, as if reflecting the sun from the sea that crashed against the cliffs below.

She led Emerick and Tig to the farthest corner of the keep where the inner curtain wall met the keep's wall on the edge of the cliff.

"This is where Celestria used to go with your father," Emerick said, his voice hushed.

"Aye, Da told me. That's why I brought you here, because she'd be proud of you for this." Drest ran her hand over the stones on the wall, the ridges and mortar. "Emerick, do you see this?"

"Do I see what?" He cleared his throat. "Did your father say there's something wrong with the stones?"

"Nay, it's not wrong. Put your fingers in these ridges. Nay, not there, up here." She pointed above her head.

Emerick obeyed. "Is this worse than what's below?"

"Put your foot there and see. Aye, right there. Go ahead."

Emerick stepped onto the lower stone, supporting himself with his grip from above. "I don't feel any difference."

"Reach up as high as you can. Aye, that's right. Now move your foot up."

"What am I trying to find, Drest? What was it that you wanted to show me?"

"Do you have a good grip? Look down."

He did, and his eyes widened. "I—Drest, I'm going to fall. Quickly, please call Wulfric—"

"Nay, lad, just keep your fingers and your feet where they are." In seconds, she'd climbed up beside him. "Emerick, do you not see?"

He swallowed. "Do I not see what?"

"That you're climbing a wall. I thought you should learn."

He studied her, his mouth an uneasy line. "Are you *sure* this is a good idea? You won't let me fall, will you?"

"You won't fall."

Tig began to hum a soft triumphant tune. Mordag rose higher, soaring toward the tower.

"Put your hand up here, next to mine," Drest said. "Are you ready?"

"God's bones, I hope so."

"Here we go, then."

Drest waited until his fingers were firm upon his new grip, and showed him where to step next.

At the battlements stands the guard of this hall,
her sword in her hand, her eye on the road;
a lady in title, but a warrior withal.
Our tales of adventure, of this lady they bode,
of her bravery and kindness and goodness they bode.

Yet—be wary of what this Madwulf will do
if you dare to threaten the castle's young lord;
You'll know well the scratch of the knife that she threw
Or the glittering silver, the whoosh of her sword:
Aye, you'll hear the song of that blade, her own mighty
sword.

—*Anonymous, AD 1210, Faintree Castle*

Code of the Mad Wolf's War-Band:

Shuttle your courage back and forth with someone
you trust.

Always carry a weapon.

Never falter before yourself or the enemy.

Accept no defeat: Always fight.

Honor and protect all matrons and maidens.

Drest's Codes:

Sometimes only words can save you.

Rely on the strength of matrons and maidens.

⟿ Glossary ⟿

Arrow loop: A narrow opening or slit in a castle's wall or battlement, used to fire arrows from within.

Bailey: The inner yard of a castle, between a defensive wall and the inner tower.

Bairn (Scots language, pronounced *BERN*): "Child."

Battlement: The top of a castle wall or tower, usually featuring spaced openings through which its warriors fight.

Beck (Scots language): A stream.

Bolt: What a crossbow shoots: a small, straight, cylindrical piece of wood with a metal point.

Caudle: A healing drink, often with made with oats, other grains, or bread, as well as eggs, and spices.

Crenel: The gaps between the stone merlons atop a battlement.

Crossguard (part of a sword): A horizontal piece of metal on the hilt above the blade that protects the hand on the grip.

Curtain wall: The defensive outer wall of a castle, made of stone and mortar. These were tall and usually seven or more feet thick.

Grip (part of a sword): The middle part of the hilt between the pommel and the crossguard; it's what you hold.

Hauberk (pronounced: *HALL-berk*): A shirt of chain mail that covers the neck, shoulders, arms, and chest, and reaches past the hips.

Hilt (part of a sword): The entire top section of a sword (everything that comes above the blade itself).

Inner bailey: The fortified inner wall of a castle directly before the tower or keep.

Keep: The inner building or tower of a castle, protected by outer fortifications, and thus its safest place.

Merlon: The thick square pieces atop a battlement.

Midden: A heap of refuse (including rotting plants and human waste). A medieval compost pile, more or less.

Murder holes: Found usually around the entries or gatehouses of castles, these holes in the stone allowed defenders to dump rather horrible things upon the invaders below: from rocks to boiling water to, worst of all, hot sand, which would get through the chinks of chain mail and hurt considerably. (Dumping boiling oil on enemies is a myth, by the way; it was far too expensive for most British castles to care to waste it in this way.)

Pommel (part of a sword): The shaped end of a sword's hilt, which sits above the hand, which serves as a counter-weight.

Postern gate: A small, fortified back door of a castle, built into the curtain wall, providing an emergency escape for defenders who needed to flee. The door was too narrow for an army to enter, so they were not of use for a castle's whole garrison, just a handful of people, such as the lord and his guards.

Siege engine: A wooden or wood-and-metal structure like a trebuchet, mangonel, or battering ram used to siege a castle.

Solar: The safest bedchamber in a castle keep, usually built near the top, used by the rulers of the castle.

Surcoat: A long, loose, sleeveless garment worn over chain mail, reaching the knees, usually with a heraldic emblem on the front (Faintree Castle's is a blue tree).

⊷ Author's Note ⊷

In 1210, Scotland hadn't reached what most people consider its most dramatic period of history. Yes, there were wee battles going on, and the Scottish throne would soon be challenged. But in about a century, the Wars of Scottish Independence would be at hand with Robert the Bruce, the famous Scottish warrior king, at the helm. In Lord Faintree's day, however, the Lowlands of Scotland—along the Borders and up a bit—was a somewhat quiet place, which is why I chose this political setting for Drest's story. I wanted to avoid the drama of Robert the Bruce's times in order to delve deep into my own characters' worlds and allow their adventures to thrive—and not be limited by the happenings of important wars.

A Lord's or Lady's Role

This period had many things in common with other times of medieval Scottish history. It had feudalism and rule of law. As in other places in Britain in the early thirteenth century, feudalism meant that a leader like Lord Faintree or Lady de Moys could demand annual goods or services from the people who lived on the swaths of land that the lord or lady owned. Goods came in the form of grain or crops. Services sometimes came in the form of men for battle, which is why Emerick is so distraught when Grimbol demands service from Phearsham Ridge. Demanding such a service was a lord's privilege—and Grimbol had no right to require it.

Demanding service from the men of a village was one way to amass an army. Villagers would have been armed with weapons like homemade spears and armor of leather, but never swords (more on that later) or chain mail (which was extremely expensive). During times of war, a lord or lady would compose a good chunk of his or her army from such village soldiers. But they could also keep a significant army of hired soldiers at hand, if they had the money. Knights without land would also serve at the castle. A distinguished knight like Sir Reynard was no doubt paid well for his service, which involved living at the castle and working closely with the army.

Powerful Women

While Lord Faintree has some means, he has very little in comparison with Lady de Moys. That lady is not only very wealthy but also the most powerful person in this book. It wasn't uncommon for someone connected to

Scottish royalty to also have connections with French royalty; for centuries, the Scots and the French were allies of varying levels, brought together against the common enemy of the English. It was unusual, though, for a woman to have the kind of power that Lady de Moys has—unusual, but not entirely unheard of. I imagined Lady de Moys as a brilliant statesman, able to command loyalty from her home army in Scotland but also her husband's army in France. During her husband's life, she would have grown to know the men of her armies, its leaders but also its trained soldiers. She would have shown herself a good listener, and brave, and able to stand the sight of blood, perhaps even tending wounds when the men returned from battle. After her husband died, she would have been generous to his supporters, rewarded his most loyal men well, and listened to them. In that way, I can imagine her winning them over.

Noblewomen, even ones like Lady de Moys, didn't typically don armor and go to battle, but a woman might lead her men in a battle, though she'd keep in the back when the fight began. By being charismatic and courageous, a woman leader could make a difference. The courage of such a leader has been known to inspire an army to victory. A few such experiences like this would have bonded Lady de Moys very closely with her army.

Marriage and Power

Unfortunately, most noblewomen—in particular, young noblewomen—were at the command of their older male relatives when it came to the men they married. Neither Celestria nor Oriana had a choice. Marriages were alliances meant to strengthen the family. And as Emerick described, lords like the old Lord Faintree (and Lord Harkniss, Oriana's father) would use their children's marriages to attain a position of importance for themselves. Sometimes this could go far: When there wasn't a clear successor to a throne—and you never knew when an heir would die in battle or from illness—the people closest to the throne would have a chance of reaching that throne (that's what happened with Robert the Bruce). If not that, they'd at least receive more lands, which meant more power. It really was a brilliant strategy on the old Lord Faintree's part to marry off his two children to people with such links to the French and Scottish thrones as Lord de Moys and Oriana Harkniss. Too bad for him that Celestria wasn't about to stand for it, and that old Lord Harkniss saw Lord de Moys as a better catch than the four-year-old Emerick.

Allies

Marriages could lead to powerful alliances, but old friendships could as well. Emerick is fortunate that the

Harkniss and Faintree families have always been friendly even without a marriage. Thanks to Celestria, Oriana considers him a close friend and ally, and is willing to lend him her men. Usually an ally wouldn't be willing to assist in what was essentially a family dispute. Most would have waited to see who would end up on top, Emerick or Oswyn.

Medieval Law and Order

This period in medieval times saw laws much like laws today, prohibiting crimes like theft or murder. And there was law enforcement. For small towns like Phearsham Ridge, the community as a whole or its leader (someone like Arnulf) enforced laws, and would come to a consensus if the crime was small and could be easily settled. If someone had committed a serious crime, the perpetrator would be taken to the town's lord or lady, who would serve as judge. A lord or lady heard complaints, then convicted (or not), and sentenced. This was the point of Lady de Moys's Petition Day; often, a lord or lady would admit his or her people into the castle at set times to hear disagreements, requests, and cases. If the crime was committed against the lord or lady (such as stealing from the lord's forests or lands), the punishment was dire: Thieves could expect to lose a hand for poaching, or even be hanged if the stolen goods were valuable (such as a horse). Sentences were entirely up to the lord or lady.

A wolf's head was a dire sentence. It was also rare; lords would use it only for the most dangerous and elusive outlaws. It meant just what Emerick described: that anyone who saw the person thus sentenced had the right to execute that person (medieval law prohibited people from going about slaying each other, so this was quite unusual). A wolf's head didn't always come with a generous reward; Sir Oswyn was clearly putting everything he could into slaying a person he deemed as the most dangerous in the lowlands (at least to his interests).

Scottish Currency

In 1210, Scotland didn't have a currency that was widely used. Later in the thirteenth century, kings would stamp and issue their own silver coins, but in the time and place depicted in this book, people commonly used English silver coins. The currency was the pound, determined by a literal pound of silver pennies. It was common in Scotland, especially in rural areas like the setting of this story, for people to trade goods for other goods rather than use coins.

But for those who did use coins, thirty pounds was a lot. It was what a lord would pay to buy a fine horse, for instance. (Think of it as akin to the price of a really fancy car.) That's an unusual bounty on a girl's head, but, like the wolf's head sentence, just shows how much Oswyn viewed Drest as a threat, and how much he wanted her slain—and how much he worried that a lass who could escape his castle's prison might well elude all his men.

Knighthood

Knighthood was bestowed in three different ways: on a battlefield after a courageous act, before a battle as a means of giving a young and untested man courage, or in a lavish ceremony. No one inherited a knighthood during this period: Even a knight's son had to earn it.

But a knight's son would be led toward a knighthood from a young age. At seven or eight, a boy would become a page at a castle and serve the lord and lady; then at fourteen or fifteen become a squire and still serve the castle, but also start practicing battle techniques (fighting with practice swords and shields, jousting with a target, riding a horse with a weapon, and working up the muscles to be able to mount a horse in full armor); and then at twenty-one (though sometimes a knight would be younger) he would undergo a ceremony.

This ceremony would start with an overnight vigil in the castle's chapel during which the knight-to-be would meditate on the great responsibility of being a knight—a responsibility to his lord, to God (this was a Christian ceremony), and to his family's honor. In the morning, he'd take a hot bath, then dress in a long white tunic, symbolizing cleansing and purity, a kind of rebirth. The ceremony would take place in front of the entire castle and would include language much like the kind that Emerick uses. At the end, a knight would receive a sword and a pair of spurs.

Women did not receive honors like this. They acquired titles like "lady" through birth or marriage. It would have been highly unusual for anyone to knight a girl, but I like to think that a lord could have done it if he'd wanted. He'd make a great many knights angry, though, because knighthood was a serious and elite honor.

Swords

I promised more on swords earlier, so here's a bit about the sword in relation to knights: Only knights were permitted to carry swords. Men-at-arms carried long daggers, battle-axes, or spears. Even squires weren't allowed to carry a real sword in battle until they were knighted. That Grimbol has trained all his children to fight with swords and given them real swords shows his flagrant defiance of this rule of medieval life.

Literacy

It may have surprised some readers that Tig, the cleverest person in the book, can't read or write. Neither can Drest or her brothers, or Grimbol. Literacy was an elite skill. Castle pages were taught how to read. Some villagers might have their children taught by the local priest, but during this time, most didn't. This is one example of the differences that Tig, Drest, and her family will find between themselves and the other castle warriors-in-training. But it's a skill they're all going to learn.

⊰ Acknowledgments ⊱

This sequel to *The Mad Wolf's Daughter* has evolved as a whole new quest. Just like in the book, I've been accompanied by many of my companions from the last time, as well as some new friends.

One of my most crucial companions, the Tig to my Drest, is my son, Benjamin, whose advice on every draft ensured that the plot made sense, the language was clear, and the story moved swiftly. It's meant a lot to have you as my first editor and also my most enthusiastic fan—and I love that I've written much of this novel with you here in the same room, quietly reading, always ready to put down your book to listen to and critique a sentence. Many thanks also to my husband, Michael, who has been an incredible support every step of the way: reading drafts, listening to me talk over plot points at dinner and breakfast, and simply being proud of this book and of me. You're the Emerick to my Drest.

Thank you to my editor, Kathy Dawson, whose brilliant touch has helped me yet again take Drest's story to new heights. Your advice, suggestions, and blunt challenges are like Drest's brothers combined: You helped me figure out how to make this tale shine as it always should have. (I don't know how I'd have reached this point without you!)

Thank you to Antonio Javier Caparo for another piece of incredible cover art, this time with all the characters I love most on the front and back! They're perfect, and I'm lucky to have you as my ally in this endeavor. Thank you also to Maggie Edkins for your fantastic work on the design—and to Sophie E. Tallis for drawing another marvelous map.

So many people in publishing helped with this book. Thanks especially to the Penguin Young Readers team: my marvelous publicist Lily Yengle, who seems to always know exactly what's going on everywhere at every time; Susie Albert, Judy Samuels; and to Regina Castillo and Mina Chung, who both did so much to make these pages beautiful. And to my agent, Adriann Ranta Zurhellen: Thank you for being there when I needed you most.

I'm also grateful to the students, teachers, and school librarians I've presented to (in person and by Skype) who have been such champions of my work: Julia Colvin at Mast Landing Elementary, Monica Moorman at Orange Brook Elementary, Katie Reilley at Blackberry Creek Elementary, Meg Rooks at Lyman Moore Middle School, and Alison Snow at Creek View Elementary. Also many thanks to the bookstore staff who have shown such enthusiasm for my work (with special thanks to Gibran Graham at The Briar Patch, Kenny Brechner at DDG Booksellers, and Stephanie Heinz at Print: A Bookstore).

Thank you to the medieval scholars who have made researching this book so pleasant with the fascinating resources you've made easily available in print and online. Many thanks especially to David Santiuste (University of Edinburgh) for his work as well as his help with a last-minute query about currency.

Finally, thank you to all my readers. I hope that this chapter in Drest's adventures entertained, delighted, and inspired you. Thank you for joining me on this journey.

Read on for the
wee lass's first adventure

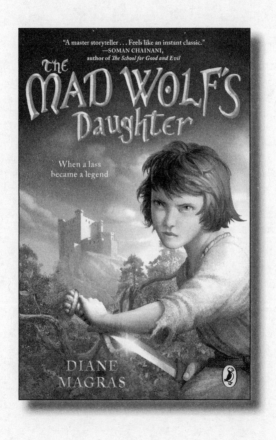

~« 1 »~

THE SHAPE IN THE WATER

The fog drew back upon the dark sea and revealed a gleaming point like a ship's bow, which seemed to nod at the girl brooding by the glowing bonfire.

"What's that?" Drest leaned forward, her hand on her dagger.

Her elbow dug into the shoulder of her brother Gobin, who lay with his arm slung over the fringe of his coal-black hair.

"Gobin?" She poked him. "Are you awake?"

"Nay."

"There's something in the sea."

"I'm not awake, lass."

"It's something wooden on the waves just past the dragons' teeth."

His eyes flicked open, then closed. "Drest, dear, it's a dream. Lie back. If you want to stay out here with us, you need to sleep."

1

Drest crept around the fire to Nutkin, Gobin's twin, who lay in almost the same position, except it was his hand, not arm, that held back his black hair.

"I'm not awake, either," Nutkin said, a smile tweaking his lips.

"We come home from war and you're jumping at every sound," muttered Uwen, her youngest brother. "Go to sleep, you crab-headed squid gut, or I'll make you sleep in the cave with the snails."

Drest crawled back to the water's edge. The sea was quiet. The night mist had swept in again. She listened, unmoving, the wind's fingers riffling her short and uneven brown hair.

Grimbol, her father, had always said that no boat or ship could reach their tight, protected cove, that the dragons' teeth—the stones scattered over the harbor—were hungry for wood and men. And no man or devil would dare draw near the headland while her brothers and father were home.

Yet something was there.

Drest left the circle by the fire where her family slept and scrambled up the boulders behind the camp. She climbed over the crumbling stones, dead tree roots, and clumps of gorse, past the crag that looked over the spot of rocky beach where her brothers kept their boats, then higher, until she came to a point where the sea opened up before the headland. Above her rose the path to the cliffs. Behind her lay the caves where her family kept their supplies and slept when it rained. Over the water, the ash-gray fog stretched like smoke. Drest closed her eyes and listened.

Waves, sloshing.

The wind, gently breathing.

Her father and brothers, snoring from below.

A creak.

Not just a creak, but a scrape as well, the rasp of wood on stone in the cove just past the dragons' teeth. She knew that sound: a boat. And it was landing.

Drest flew down the uneven cliff side, blind in the darkness but knowing her way. She pounded back into the camp toward the glow of the bonfire, and dropped to her knees beside her eldest brother.

"Wulfric, there's a boat in the water!"

Wulfric opened his eyes a crack. "What are you saying, lass?"

"A boat. Like one of yours! Lads, get up!"

Heads rose around her. Her father turned over with a growl.

"Our poor wee Drest's had a nightmare," murmured Thorkill, fingering the stone pendant he wore below his curly ginger beard. "Was it Gobin's battle story that kept you awake, lass?"

3

"Nay, it's not that! I heard a boat." Drest stood, wincing at her brothers' shaking heads. "Lads, I *saw* it!"

"Keep your grub-spotted nightmares to yourself," Uwen mumbled from beside the fire.

Her brothers settled down again, grunting and grumbling, until she was standing alone.

"Why won't you listen? Do I ever tell stories? Lads, there's a *boat* out there."

No one spoke.

Drest opened her mouth, but before she could say anything more, the camp was bright with flames.

⤙ 2 ⤚

INVADERS

They rushed from the shadows, men with massive swords and gleaming shields, their bucket-shaped helms hiding their faces.

Drest's brothers always slept beside their weapons, and were up and armed in seconds, but the invaders had gained an advantage. Nutkin ducked behind the fire and slid to avoid a blade. Wulfric fought from his knees and battered away the enemy who had fallen upon him. Shields crashed together. Swords shrieked against chain mail.

In the middle of it stood Drest, far from her practice sword on the other side of the fire.

A knight dropped his sword and slumped against her. Drest scrambled out from under him, and slammed into another knight's shield, emblazoned with a tree, just like Wulfric's battered one. Drest ducked, twisted, and crawled away. On the loose rocks by the path, she panted. She had never seen a battle, and the sight of it squeezed like an iron band around her chest.

An unfamiliar grasp clamped onto her shoulder.

Drest gave a cry and tried to plunge back into the fight, but an arm gleaming with chain mail grabbed her around the waist and dragged her away, up the path. She lashed out, kicking nothing but rocks and air.

Her captor stumbled. Drest clawed at the stones, then at the hilt of a sword someone had dropped. Her fingers closed on the grip and she swung the blade back. A heavy note rang low and muted against the mail on the man's legs.

"So even a wee wolf like you has teeth." The knight swung down his shield, knocking Drest's sword from her hand.